"I don't go to dinner v

"What, you only go out with boring guys?" Dylan Smith asked.

In spite of Charlotte's attempts to stifle it, she couldn't help laughing. "Sorry."

"Have dinner with me anyway," he insisted. "You can tell me about Sturgeon Falls. Background for my story."

She was tempted. And that surprised her. She had a hard-and-fast rule about getting involved with tourists, and that included reporters from Green Bay.

Seeing her hesitation, he pressed. "You can pick the place, and I'll meet you there."

"All right," she finally said, hoping she wouldn't regret it.

Why had she agreed to meet him? She knew nothing about him. And he hadn't been completely truthful with her, judging by the way he'd avoided her eyes.

She should be old enough, and experienced enough, to see through a charmer like Dylan Smith.

Apparently she wasn't as immune to charming men as she'd thought....

Dear Reader,

I really enjoyed writing Dylan and Charlotte's story. Dylan was a secondary character in *Small-Town Secrets*, and I just couldn't let him go. And although Charlotte appeared in only one short scene in the same book, I knew immediately that I wanted to write a book about her. Female charter-boat captains are rare, and I wanted to explore what kind of woman would enjoy this tough, physical job.

Dylan and Charlotte's story is about family, about how much we hunger for connections. Families aren't always bound together by blood ties—they can be created, as well. And sometimes the families we create for ourselves have the strongest bonds.

I hope you enjoy Dylan and Charlotte's story and their exploration of what makes a family.

I love to hear from my readers. E-mail me at mwatson1004@hotmail.com or visit my Web site at www.margaretwatson.com.

Margaret Watson

SMALL-TOWN FAMILY

Margaret Watson

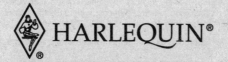

TORONTO • NEW YORK • LONDON
AMSTERDAM • PARIS • SYDNEY • HAMBURG
STOCKHOLM • ATHENS • TOKYO • MILAN • MADRID
PRAGUE • WARSAW • BUDAPEST • AUCKLAND

ISBN-13: 978-0-373-71420-9
ISBN-10:   0-373-71420-3

SMALL-TOWN FAMILY

Printed in U.S.A.

ABOUT THE AUTHOR

Margaret Watson has always made up stories in her head. When she started actually writing them down, she realized that she'd found exactly what she wanted to do with the rest of her life. Fifteen years after staring at that first blank page, she's written eighteen books for Silhouette and Harlequin Books.

When she's not writing or spending time with her family, she practices veterinary medicine. Besides the tremendous satisfaction in her job, it provides the inspiration for wonderful characters and interesting stories. Margaret lives in a Chicago suburb with her husband and three daughters and a menagerie of pets.

Don't miss any of our special offers. Write to us at the following address for information on our newest releases.

Harlequin Reader Service
U.S.: 3010 Walden Ave., P.O. Box 1325, Buffalo, NY 14269
Canadian: P.O. Box 609, Fort Erie, Ont. L2A 5X3

This is for my family—my sister, Nancy Good, and my brothers, John and Dan Watson, my mother, Lenore Watson, and in memory of my father, Tom Watson.

And thanks to Scott Osborne of RV Charters in Algoma, Wisconsin, for his insight into charter fishing—and for all the salmon we caught!

CHAPTER ONE

"WHAT DO YOU THINK you're doing?"

The floating pier dipped and swayed beneath Dylan's feet as a woman leaped from a boat and ran toward him. The sun glinted off something large and shiny in her fist.

Dylan instinctively stepped backward, but the woman ignored him as she jumped onto another boat. Moments later, two young men scrambled out of it.

"Stop them," the woman shouted to Dylan.

Dylan tried to block them in the middle of the narrow pier, but they didn't slow down. Dylan grabbed at the first one, but his hand slid off the kid's slippery track jacket. The boy twisted, using his shoulder to knock Dylan off balance, then threw an elbow at Dylan's face. He tasted blood as the second boy shoved him against a post. By the time he regained his footing, they were past him.

As he turned to chase them, the woman flashed past, holding a huge wrench. She didn't spare him a glance.

Before Dylan could catch up he heard the sound of motors revving and gravel spitting in the parking lot. He reached it in time to see the woman fling the wrench onto the ground.

She stood with her hands on her hips, watching the two boys zoom out of the parking lot on dirt bikes. Sun glittered off the metal lying at her feet.

"You want to follow them?" he asked. "My car is right here."

"Forget it," she said with disgust. She kicked at the wrench and it spun on the gravel. "We can't drive a car down the bike path."

"What was that all about?"

The woman bent to pick up the tool. "They were trashing one of the boats," she said. "Thanks for trying to stop them."

"Didn't do much good, did I?"

"You tried," she said, shoving her hair out of her eyes, and he got his first good look at her.

Her blond hair, falling out of a ponytail, looked streaked by the sun and tousled by the wind. Anger still burned in her bright blue eyes. Her knuckles were white as she gripped the wrench.

He'd seen her before. He frowned as he tried to remember where.

She scowled. "Why are you staring at me?"

"I know you."

"I've never seen you before."

"I'm Dylan Smith," he said, sucking on the inside of his lip as he held out his hand.

She hesitated before taking it. "Charlotte Burns."

"I saw you at Kendall Van Allen's house," he said, smiling and remembering his glimpse of the blonde in the pickup truck and the kick of interest she'd inspired. "You were leaving as I was arriving. I asked Kendall who you were."

"You know Kendall?" She pulled her hand away from him, still wary.

"I'm staying at Van Allen House."

The tension in her shoulders eased and she smiled ruefully. "A tourist. Great. This isn't the image of Door County we're going for."

"Yeah, I'm shocked. I've never seen kids acting like knuckleheads before."

"This was more than a prank," Charlotte said as she started back toward the pier. "If I hadn't heard them, they could have done serious damage to Gus's boat."

"Gus?" Dylan hurried after her. "Gus Macauley?"

She stopped and looked at him. "You know Gus?"

"No, but I'm looking for him."

"He's not here."

"I gathered as much when you said those kids were on his boat," he said, unable to keep the impatience out of his voice. "Do you know how to get in touch with him?"

"Doesn't matter. Gus is unavailable."

"What are you? His secretary?" Frustration and anger boiled up inside him. He pulled out a tissue and wiped his mouth impatiently. It had taken him far too long to get this lead. Gus Macauley was one of the few people still around who had worked with

Stuart Van Allen. And now this woman was trying to keep him away from Macauley.

Her gaze drilled a hole through him. "I'm his…" She clamped her mouth shut. "I'm a friend of his family," she finally said.

"What's going on? Is he out of town?"

She studied him and he stared right back, not giving an inch. He'd thought she was attractive when he'd seen her outside of Van Allen House. Close up, she was striking, with high cheekbones and huge eyes. But now he could see the steel beneath the beautiful surface.

"Who are you?" she asked.

"Dylan Smith."

"I remember your name. What do you want with Gus?"

"That's between Mr. Macauley and me."

"Fine. I'll tell him you were looking for him."

"It's business. I need to ask him some questions."

Her hand tightened on the wrench. "Did those developers send you? Did you set this whole thing up? Send those kids to vandalize his boat, then conveniently show up in time to chase them?" She stepped closer. "Did you deliberately get in my way to keep me from catching them?"

He sucked at the bloodied inside of his lip. "Oh, yeah, this was planned. Especially the blood. Makes it more realistic."

"You're bleeding?" She scanned his face, dropping the wrench and leaning toward him when she saw his lip. "Let me see."

"It's nothing. The kid caught me with his elbow."

"Your lip is swelling." She reached out to touch it, then stopped. "I'm sorry. Let me get you some ice."

"I don't need ice," he said, waving her away. "I need to know what you're talking about. What developers? What's going on?"

She sighed. "Sorry. I'm jumping to conclusions—we've all been tense. You *did* try to stop those kids."

She started down the pier, leaving him standing where he was. After a few steps, she turned around. "Do you want some ice, or not?"

"I don't need ice," he said, following. "Tell me about the developers. What's going on?"

"Never mind. It's a long, boring story for anyone besides the charter captains."

"Trust me," he said. "I won't think it's boring."

When he reached the boat the boys had been on, Dylan saw the debris scattered around the deck. Fishing poles were broken into small pieces, seat cushions were ripped open and a window in the cabin was smashed.

"My God," he said. "Those two kids did all this?"

"And they weren't even here that long," she said. "It's a good thing I was on my boat and heard them."

"You have a boat here?" He looked around. "Aren't these all fishing boats?"

"Yes and yes," she said, stepping aboard. She opened the door and disappeared into the cabin. A few moments later she was back with a plastic bag of ice.

Dylan set it on the rail and watched as she picked up a cushion and centered it on the cooler tucked into a corner of the deck, smoothing her palm over it. He pulled out his notebook and scribbled a few notes, then shoved the notebook back into his pocket. He ignored the ice. "Can I help you clean up this mess?"

"That's very kind of you." Her mouth curved. "Especially considering how rude I've been."

He stared. "You should smile more," he managed to say. "It's a good look for you."

"Right." She rolled her eyes. "Thanks for your help, Mr. Smith. I'll tell Gus you were looking for him."

It was clearly a dismissal. "I'm serious. Let me help you with this."

Her smile disappeared. "I can't clean it up yet," she said. "The police need to see it and I have to take pictures for the insurance company."

"Then I'll wait for the police with you."

"Not necessary. But thanks for offering."

"You said you were on your boat when you heard those kids. Are you a fishing guide?"

"I am. Is that why you were looking for Gus? Did you want to book a charter?"

"No. But maybe I'll change my mind. You're not what I expected in a guide."

She shook her head, but Dylan saw a flicker of response in her eyes. "That's lame, Smith. And not very original. You think that's the first time I've heard that line?"

"Maybe not, but I'm sincere."

"Right. And I just fell off the turnip truck yester-day."

He grinned. He was going to enjoy talking to Charlotte Burns. "You doubt me? I'm crushed."

"Yeah, I can see that. What are you doing here, Smith? What do you want?"

Dylan hesitated, then he pulled his wallet out of his pocket and opened it. "I'm a reporter for the *Green Bay News-Gazette,*" he said. "I'm working on a story and I hoped Gus could give me some information."

Charlotte glanced at the man standing on the pier. She'd felt a flash of familiarity when she saw him. Had she seen him at Kendall's? It didn't matter. She didn't care for the twinge of attraction she felt. His longish, dark-blond hair framed a handsome face with a dimple in his right cheek. His green eyes examined her carefully, as if he was memorizing her.

The leather wallet was warm in her hand, and Charlotte glanced down at the picture on his employee ID. His hair was shorter, but the dimple in his right cheek showed up clearly, even in the grainy photo.

Snapping the wallet shut, she handed it back to him. "What kind of story are you working on?"

"I came here for the dedication of the high school football field to Carter Van Allen. But as I researched the piece, I changed the focus to the history of the Van Allen orchard. I'm not sure where it will end up."

He flipped through the pages of his notebook. Too quickly. "Can you tell me how to get hold of Gus?"

What did this guy really want with Gus? "He'll be back in a week or two." She picked up an unbroken fishing pole and set it inside the cabin's sliding glass door. "Thanks for your help earlier, but I have things to do."

"Can you spare another couple of minutes?" he asked. "To answer a few questions?"

"About what?"

"The orchard. Any memories you have of it."

His gaze didn't quite meet hers, and her stomach tightened again. This time with caution instead of attraction. "Why on earth would you think I have any connection to the orchard? How can I possibly help you?"

"Kendall said you were Carter's cousin. Didn't you spend time at Van Allen House when you were younger?"

"My mother and Carter's mother were sisters. So yes, I was there."

"How often?"

Charlotte crossed her arms and watched him, wary. "Often enough."

"What does that mean?"

"It means they were relatives, and we saw them." She caught herself when she heard her voice rising. "How much time did you spend time with your relatives when you were a kid?"

"Not enough." His hand tightened on his pen. "What can you tell me about Stuart Van Allen?"

She shrugged. "Stuart? Nothing. I didn't know him. He was always at the orchard. My mother went to see her sister." To ask for money. The remembered shame still made her throat constrict.

"Did you hang around with Carter?"

"He was five years older than me. What do you think?"

He looked up with a disarming twinkle in his eyes. "I'll bet you followed him around like a puppy dog. And he wouldn't spare you a glance."

"Pretty much." She stared out at the water, unwilling to succumb to his charm. "Gabe Townsend was always nice to me, though."

"Did you know Townsend is back?"

Charlotte relaxed, remembering the attraction that she'd seen between Gabe and Kendall. "Yes. I saw him last time I was at Kendall's place."

"It's getting awfully sloppy and sentimental over there," Smith said. "I think they're getting married. And Townsend has only been here for a couple of weeks."

"Really? That's great." She smiled at Smith's pained expression. "I take it you don't believe in love at first sight."

Smith snorted. "Please." His gaze warmed as he looked at her. "But I could make an exception for you."

"Wow," she said lightly, although her heart fluttered. "Lucky me."

"You have no idea."

Charlotte couldn't help grinning back at him. "I like humility in a man."

"Really? I always thought humility was overrated."

Charlotte stood. "Are you always this cocky, Smith?"

"It's Dylan. And I'm actually very shy. You're bringing me out of my shell."

"Is that right?" She examined him. "You don't seem like the shy and retiring type to me."

He blinked innocently. "Didn't anyone ever tell you appearances can be deceiving?"

He was a charmer, all right. But she'd already been inoculated against charm. "I can't help you."

"So you don't remember anything about Stuart?"

"Sorry. I didn't spend much time with him. Why are you focusing on Stuart?"

"He owned one of the largest orchards in the county, so he's the logical starting point. I'm interested in the history of the industry. The owners, the orchards. The migrant workers."

Charlotte straightened. "Is that what this is about? The migrants? Are you writing an ugly piece about the miserable lives they endure? Because if you are, you can leave right now. Kendall goes way beyond what's legally and morally required. And so did Stuart."

"I'm not trying to hurt anyone." He carefully shut his notebook. "Are you always this defensive?"

She caught his notebook before he could put it away and held on. "Someone wrote a nasty story about the orchards and the migrants a few years ago that caused a lot of bad feelings up here. Kendall works hard to do the right thing for her employees."

"I'm not investigating Kendall," he answered, slowly pulling the book away from her. "I'm more interested in Stuart. Did he spend a lot of time in the office of the orchard? Or did he get outside and work with his employees? Did he get to know them?"

"I have no idea. I just know he spent a lot of time there." It had been the main subject of her Aunt Joan's complaints, and her mother had been quick to offer sympathy. Apparently it had worked, because her mother usually left Van Allen House clutching a handful of money.

"Do you remember anyone else who worked there?"

She stared at him, suddenly uneasy. "I was a kid. Why would I know who worked there?"

"Doesn't Gus talk about it?"

"Gus is a fisherman. He never worked in the orchard."

"Actually, he did. Bertie gave me his name."

"The orchard manager said Gus worked there?" She frowned. "He must have confused Gus with someone else."

"Yeah? It sounds like you know Gus pretty well. What else can you tell me about him?"

"That you're on the wrong track. He's a fisherman. Always has been. I have a charter—" she glanced at her watch "—in forty minutes. I really don't have time to play games with you right now."

He stood and shoved the notebook into his pocket. "How about this evening?"

She raised her eyebrows. "I'm not interested in

playing games with you anytime." Okay, maybe she was a little interested. But she didn't want to be.

"I meant can we talk again this evening?" he said. "Can I buy you dinner?"

"I won't be back until late."

"I'll wait."

"I don't go to dinner with strange men," she said.

"What? You only go out with boring guys?"

In spite of her attempts to stifle it, a bubble of laughter escaped. "I can't tell you anything more about the orchard or Stuart Van Allen. Sorry."

"Have dinner with me anyway. You can tell me about Sturgeon Falls. Background for my story."

She was tempted. And that surprised her. She had a hard-and-fast rule about getting involved with tourists, and that included reporters from Green Bay.

Seeing her hesitation, he pressed. "You can pick the place and I'll meet you there."

"All right," she said, hoping she wouldn't regret it. "I guess I owe you one for trying to stop those kids. I'll meet you at the Nightingale Supper Club." She gave him directions. "About nine o'clock."

"I'll be there."

She watched as he jumped off the boat and headed down the pier. When he reached the end, he turned and waved.

Irritated that he'd caught her watching, she headed to her own boat. Why had she agreed to meet him? She knew nothing about him. And he hadn't been completely truthful with her, judging by the way he'd avoided her eyes.

She tossed the wrench into her toolbox, disgusted with herself. She should be old enough, and experienced enough, to see through a charmer like Smith.

Apparently she wasn't as immune to charming men as she'd thought.

CHAPTER TWO

SMOKE HUNG IN A BLUE HAZE above the bar of the Nightingale Supper Club and wove around the heads of the patrons sitting there. Listening to snatches of conversation that drifted past him, Dylan took a drink of his cold, smooth beer and glanced around the crowded room.

A few tourists stood out, with their sunburned faces and backward ball caps. Some of them still had their cameras dangling around their necks. Everyone was friendly to them, but it was clear they were outsiders.

Dylan guessed that the majority clustered at the bar were locals. They had an attitude of familiarity with one another and the bartender. And he doubted that Charlotte spent her time in tourist places.

No, Charlotte was definitely a local, connected to both the Van Allens and Gus Macauley. Exactly the person to help him dig more deeply into Stuart Van Allen, the orchard and a woman who had worked there thirty-one years ago. The fact that Charlotte was gorgeous and interesting was a bonus.

She'd seemed awfully protective of Macauley,

he mused, staring into his beer. He wondered how she was connected to him. Macauley had to be old enough to be her father.

Were they involved? A couple? She acted as if she knew Macauley well.

He was surprised at the jealousy that bloomed inside him. And a little disturbed. Jealousy had never been one of his vices.

He was nursing his second beer and wondering if she'd changed her mind when she walked in.

He froze, his beer halfway to his mouth. Her transformation was amazing. Instead of the jeans and T-shirt she'd been wearing earlier, she wore a pair of light blue capris that emphasized her long legs and a white tank top that clung to her curves.

When she stopped to look around, he stood, waving to her. She wove her way through the crowds, exchanging greetings with a handful of people. Finally she dropped onto the bar stool next to his.

"Hi, Smith," she said. "I hope you haven't been waiting too long."

"It's okay," he said, trying not to stare. "It was worth the wait."

She looked amused. "I'm glad you're enjoying the Nightingale."

"Yeah, this place is fun, too." He let his gaze sweep over her, pleased when he saw her awareness. "You look good, Charlotte."

She raised one shoulder. "Did you think I'd show up in my work clothes?"

"Wouldn't have mattered. You'd still have looked good."

The corner of her mouth lifted. "Pretty smooth, aren't you?"

"Smooth. Yeah, that's my middle name. What would you like to drink?"

"A beer would be great."

He caught a whiff of her scent as he turned toward the bartender. Floral, with enough sharp citrus to keep it from being too sweet.

She watched him as she leaned against the bar and sipped her beer. He was good at reading people, but Charlotte Burns had him stumped. She was a very self-contained woman.

That only added to the challenge.

"How was your charter this afternoon?" he asked.

Surprise flickered across her face, as if she'd expected orchard questions right off the bat. He bit back a smile and settled against the bar himself. He liked that she underestimated him.

"It was fine," she said. "Noisy."

"Why noisy?"

"It was a couple and their two kids. Loud kids."

"Loud enough to scare the fish away?"

She grinned. "Nope. Fish are always caught on a Burns charter."

The hostess called his name, and after they were seated, Charlotte took a sip of beer and propped her elbows on the table. "How's your mouth?"

He touched his swollen lip. "It's okay. I'm drinking cold liquids to keep the swelling down."

"It hasn't stopped you from talking, that's for sure," she said. "So what do you want to know about Sturgeon Falls?"

"There's no rush. You've been working. You must be tired. Why don't we save the questions for another time."

She sat back slowly, watching him, her eyes carefully shuttered. He had no idea what she was thinking, and it was unsettling.

"I thought that was the point of this dinner," she finally said.

"It was. But I'd like to get to know you first."

"Why?"

He frowned. "Are you always so suspicious?"

"I am. I have a suspicious nature."

He glanced under the table. "Do you have that wrench with you?"

Her lips twitched. "No, I left it on the boat. Am I going to need it?"

"Not for me," he said, trying to look innocent.

"Hmm." She lifted her beer to her mouth, hiding her smile. "Maybe I should have brought it with me."

"If you're trying to intimidate me, it's working."

She laughed and set her beer on the table. "I don't think anything intimidates you, Smith."

"You'd be surprised, Charlotte."

She blinked. "Name one thing."

It was getting too personal. "Watching you run at me waving that wrench. That intimidated me."

"Good. I hope it scared the pants off those kids."

"They'll be seeing you with that bad boy in their nightmares."

"Then maybe they won't be back." She drank from her beer. By the time she put the bottle back on the table, she'd regained her self-control.

"Tell me about Gus Macauley," he said.

Her wariness was back, too. "He's a fisherman. He's run a charter service out of Sturgeon Falls for over thirty years." She shrugged. "That's about it. Gus is a straightforward guy."

"Are you dating him?"

She sat up straight. "Dating Gus? Are you out of your…" She set her beer down too hard. "You think I'm dating someone but agreed to have dinner with you?"

"That wouldn't have stopped some people."

"I don't cheat," she said, her voice cold.

"Good to know." He slouched in the chair. "So how *do* you know him?"

She picked at the label on her bottle. "I told you, I'm a friend of his family."

"And he's never talked about the orchard?"

"Nope. Bertie must be mistaken. I can't imagine Gus ever working in the orchard." She sat up straight. "What's going on, Smith? Why are you looking for him? Are you working for the developer that wants to buy the marina?"

"You mentioned a developer this afternoon. What's that about?"

Her eyes narrowed. "I'm not sure I'm buying the innocent look."

He pulled his notebook out of his pocket and set it on the table. "Look, Charlotte, I'm really a reporter. I showed you my ID card this afternoon. I'm really working on a story about the orchard."

She reached over and picked up his notebook, and he clenched his hands together in his lap to stop himself from grabbing it back. His fingers tightened as she thumbed through it. When she set it on the table again, he snatched it up and stuffed it in his pocket.

"Don't you know it's rude to look at someone's journal?" he asked, trying to keep his voice casual.

"Journal?" She raised her eyebrows. "You set it on the table. I assumed you offered it as your bona fides." She smiled. "I couldn't read it, anyway."

"Shorthand," he said, touching his pocket. "So are we straight? I don't have a hidden agenda." His conscience tweaked him, but he ignored it. "I was looking for Gus to ask him some questions about the orchard. I asked you to dinner to get some information about Sturgeon Falls. And also because you're an attractive woman. Okay?"

"All right." She smiled. "I'll hold off on the interrogation. We'll postpone the questions until after dinner. I'll let you flirt with me while we eat. And maybe I'll flirt back."

"Great," he said. Her smile made his head spin. "You'll let me know if I'm not holding up my end?"

"From what I've seen so far, I don't think you have anything to worry about," she said, her voice dry.

"You don't think I'm sincere?" He'd surprised

himself by how much he'd looked forward to seeing her.

She laughed. "I've already agreed to have dinner with you, Smith. Don't push your luck."

"So tell me about the developers."

She sighed. "A group from Illinois wants to buy the marina and the land around it for a resort and condos. The marina slips would be for luxury yachts, not fishing boats. But the charter captains have long-term contracts and unless they all agree, the marina can't kick them out. There have been a lot of arguments."

"Some of them want to sell out?"

"Some. Gus is one of the more vocal members of the group that wants to stay."

Dylan reached for his notebook again. "So the vandalism this afternoon might not have been random."

She raised an eyebrow. "You're quick."

"I'm an investigative reporter. They pay me to be suspicious."

She nodded slowly. "I wondered about those kids. Why Gus's boat? Why now? That's why I wanted to catch them." She took a drink. "I figured I could convince them to talk to me."

"I'd talk if you were holding that wrench."

"That was the idea."

"So where is Gus?" he asked, keeping his voice light.

"That's Gus's business," she said.

Frustration welled inside him. The clock was ticking on his vacation time. He'd hoped that once she got to know him, she'd quit being so protective of Macauley. "You said he'd be back in a week or two?"

"I hope so." Worry flickered across her face.

"Is he sick?"

She looked away. Too quickly. "Gus is fine."

Bingo.

"Sorry," he said. "I'll quit the interrogation." He shook his head. "I get carried away."

"I'm glad you enjoy your work," she said dryly.

"You have no idea."

An hour later as they walked out the restaurant door, his hand settled at the small of her back. Her muscles tensed, and he let her go as the door shut behind them.

The cool night air blew away the remnants of the cigarette smoke from the bar, and a million stars glittered in the sky. "Where's your car?" he asked.

"There's my truck," she said, nodding at a dark, well-worn pickup. "Thank you for dinner. I enjoyed myself."

"So did I." More than he'd expected. "Can I follow you home?"

She leaned against the fender. "Now that's just disappointing, Smith. I took you for classier than that."

"To make sure you get home safely," he said, feigning innocence. "What did you think I meant?"

She shook her head and climbed into her truck. "I'll see you around."

"Wait," he said, putting his hand on the window as she started the truck. "Someone vandalized

Macauley's boat. You're a friend of his. Did you ever think you might be a target, too?"

"I think that's a stretch. And besides, I'm not going home," she said. "But thanks anyway."

"Not going home?" Jealousy struck him again, surprising and unwelcome. "Where are you going?"

"Back to Gus's boat," she said. "I'm going to sleep on it for a couple of days. Make sure those kids don't come back."

"You shouldn't go back there alone at night. I'm following you."

"Thank you, but that's not necessary. Good night, Smith."

Before she could put the truck in gear, he'd trotted to his car and jumped in. "Don't bother trying to lose me," he said to her taillights. "I know where the damn boat is."

CHARLOTTE LEANED AGAINST her truck, waiting for him as he turned into the marina parking lot. Gravel sprayed as he braked to a stop.

"I told you not to follow me."

"I don't take direction well." He slammed his car door. "It's a character flaw."

"You're an annoying man, Smith."

"So I've been told." He scanned the cluster of boats bobbing gently on the dark water, and slung an arm around her shoulders. "It hasn't stopped me yet. Let's go take a look at that boat."

She shrugged off his arm. "I suppose I'm not going to get rid of you until we do."

"Nope," he said. "Gentlemen don't let ladies walk into potentially dangerous situations alone."

The pier swayed as they walked between the two rows of dark boats, and waves slapped softly against the hulls. A light shone weakly outside the office door, casting just enough illumination to show the marina was deserted and still.

"This place looks a lot different during the day," Dylan said in a low voice.

"It's quiet at night." She stopped at Gus's boat. Most of the debris had been swept up, and there was a piece of cardboard covering the broken window.

"What did the police say?" he asked.

"They said it was good the kids saw me," she replied, her voice tight. "They probably won't be back."

"So they didn't take you very seriously."

"No. When I asked them if they were going to investigate the developers, they did everything but pat me on the back and tell me not to worry my pretty little head."

"I hope they moved away quickly after saying that."

She nudged the boat with her toe and it rocked gently. "I didn't want to antagonize them."

"I can antagonize them for you. I'll do a story about the vandalism. The local paper would probably run it."

"You'd do that?" She turned to look at him.

"Sure. It's a good story. Investigative reporters

love anything that hints of a conspiracy." He grinned at her and got an answering smile.

"Thank you. That's a good idea." She turned and continued walking. "Do you want another beer? There were a couple left over from my charter this afternoon."

"Sounds good."

Farther down the dock they reached her boat. The stern was open, and various gadgets were attached to the back railing. Two steps up from the deck was a sliding glass door, but its smoky glass kept him from seeing inside. A flower box hung from the cabin window. Charlotte pulled out a set of keys and unlocked the door. "Have a seat," she said as she slid it open.

She stepped into the cabin and a light came on inside. There was a couch along one wall, and Dylan could make out the steering wheel at the front and a dark mass of fishing rods stacked in one corner.

Charlotte returned holding two beers and a couple of folding chairs. She handed him one of the bottles and opened the chairs.

"It's awfully quiet," he said, looking around. The thin crescent moon caused the surrounding boats to throw up grotesque shadows and reflected dim light off the water. Anyone could be concealed in the darkness, watching.

Waiting for him to leave.

"Yeah," she said, "I love it here at night."

"Is it safe to sleep here? Especially on a boat that has cardboard covering one of the windows?"

"The police were probably right," she said. "They were kids. They won't be out this late."

"That makes me feel much better."

She waved her hand. "I'll be fine, Smith."

The subject was definitely closed. He nodded at the flower box. "I like that you have plants growing on the water." The blossoms swayed in the gentle wind. "Quite the fashion statement."

She glanced toward them and smiled. "I work part-time in a flower shop. I couldn't resist putting these in." She touched one of the blossoms. "And it helps set the boat apart. I've had a few women who called and wanted to go out on the boat with the flowers."

"You run a fishing charter and work in a shop, too? And I thought *I* was an overachiever."

"No choice," she said. "It takes a while to build up a charter business. I have to eat in the meantime."

The boat swayed beneath him as he watched her. The breeze lifted her hair and ruffled her loose sweater.

"Working in a shop is about as far from running a fishing charter as you can get," he said. "So which is your passion?"

"The boat," she said, letting her gaze roam over its curves and lines. It almost looked like a caress. "I work in the flower shop only when I have to. I'm about done there until the end of the fishing season."

"How long have you had the boat?"

"Three years."

"You seem comfortable here. Like this fits you."

"It fits me perfectly. I love what I do."

The "back off" signs were up, so he hesitated. The boat dipped, momentarily blocking out the faint light from the building at the end of the pier, casting everything into darkness. He glanced down the row of boats to Gus's. It was deep in shadows. "I don't like to think of you staying here by yourself to confront vandals."

"They were kids, Smith. I can handle kids."

He suspected Charlotte could handle just about anything. "Okay, I'll butt out. I didn't mean to stick my nose into your business."

"Of course you did. But it's all right." She watched him over the beer bottle. "It's sweet that you're worried about me."

"You must have a lot of people who worry about you. What about your parents? Aren't they upset about this?"

"Not so much." She set the beer bottle down. "It's getting late and I have to be up early tomorrow. Thanks again for dinner, Smith."

"Dylan. And you're welcome." He hesitated. "I'd like to see you again."

"I'm not going to tell you about Gus," she said, but she smiled.

"Gus who?"

She smiled but said, "I don't date tourists."

"I'm not a tourist," he protested. "I'm from Green Bay."

"Same thing. You're both here for a week or two, then gone. I don't do vacation flings."

"I'm not asking for a fling." But a man could

hope, couldn't he? "Just dinner. Have dinner with me tomorrow."

"Sorry. I'm busy tomorrow."

The depth of his disappointment both surprised and unnerved him. "The night after that."

"I'll think about it. Good night. Dylan."

His name on her tongue sounded dark and seductive. He wanted to ask her to say it again, but stopped himself in time. "Good night, Charlotte."

When he reached the end of the pier, he looked back at her. She was still on the deck, picking up the beer bottles and the seat cushions. He waited until she went down the steps into the galley and closed the door behind her. Then he retreated to his car.

He started the ignition, then hesitated before shifting into gear. The marina was isolated and deserted. What if those kids *did* came back?

It wasn't his problem. Charlotte was a source of information, a connection to Gus and the Van Allens. An attractive woman he enjoyed flirting with. Nothing more. So why was he worrying about her?

Because he badly wanted any information she might have, he told himself. He was protecting his source. Nothing more.

He sat in his car, watching the pier until he found himself nodding off, jerking awake when his head dropped. Finally, when the moon set and the sky was turning pink on the horizon, he turned on the engine and headed to Van Allen House.

CHAPTER THREE

CHARLOTTE WOKE with a start when she tilted sharply to one side. Hearing footsteps on the stairs, she sat up abruptly and bumped her head. On the upper bunk. She was on a boat. She looked around, disoriented, and realized it wasn't even her own boat.

"Charlotte? What the hell are you doing here?"

A man in jeans and a flannel shirt descended into the galley. Gus. His buzz-cut gray hair seemed to vibrate, and his faded blue eyes were filled with concern. "Why are you sleeping on my boat?"

"What are *you* doing here? At—" she glanced at her watch "—seven in the morning."

"This is my boat," he said defensively. "I can be on my boat any damn time I like."

She grabbed her sweatshirt and pulled it over her T-shirt. "You're supposed to be taking it easy, Gus. Sleeping late. Resting."

"I can't get any rest in that house," he muttered. "She fusses over me. I can't take it anymore."

Charlotte hid her grin. "What did Frances say when you told her where you were going?"

He ran his hand over his hair. "I told her I was going to get some coffee and a bagel."

Gus was still a little pasty and hadn't regained all the weight he'd lost, but the bruised look was gone from his eyes. "You were really sick, you know," she said gently. "You were in the hospital for five days. It's not that easy to shake pneumonia. You shouldn't be here."

"Those doctors don't know what they're talking about."

"Kat seemed to think a lot of them."

"Of course she did. She's one of them." Gus stuck his chin out. "You going to tell on me?"

"I might mention to Kat that I saw you down here."

He scowled. "That's just mean, Charlotte. I never thought you were mean. You know she'll tell her mother. And then Frances will watch me like a hawk."

"Go home now and I'll forget I ever saw you."

Gus sat heavily on one of the benches in the galley. "I'm not staying long," he said. "I just had to see what those kids did to my boat."

"Damn it," she said. "Who told you?"

His victorious smirk made her smile. He looked like the old Gus. "You think I don't have friends down here?"

"Your 'friends' should have kept their mouths shut."

He looked around. "What was broken besides the window?"

Charlotte sighed. "Don't worry about it, Gus. I filed the police report and talked to the insurance agent. He's coming out today to take a look."

"Tell me."

"Stubborn old goat."

"Stubborn is your middle name, missy," he retorted. "So don't you get smart with me."

She saw his concern and sat next to him, taking his hand. "It wasn't that bad." She detailed the damage. "And we almost caught them."

"Who's we?" He frowned. "I thought all the other guys were out."

"They were. It was someone looking for you."

"Yeah? Who?"

"A reporter. Dylan Smith. He wanted to talk to you about a story he's writing." She stood and started the coffeemaker.

"About the developers?"

"No, but I think he's going to write a story about that, too. He said the local paper would run it." She shook her head. "I think he likes stirring things up."

"Can't hurt."

As he watched her pour two mugs of coffee, he said, "Damn it, Charlotte, why did you sleep here? What if those kids had come back?"

She picked her wrench up from the floor. "I would have chased them again. Caught them, this time."

"That was a damn fool thing to do. Don't you have any sense?" he said gruffly.

"It's a small thing, Gus. The least I can do."

"You don't have to do anything for me. I don't want you to get hurt, Charlotte." He wrapped his arms around her, holding her tightly, and she rested her cheek against his.

"I'm not going to get hurt," she said. "You should worry about those boys."

Gus snorted. "You talk tough, but I know what a softie you really are."

"Don't tell anyone," she said, nudging his foot with hers. "You'll ruin my image."

"You shouldn't have stayed here last night," he said. "You're much more important than this boat."

"Thank you, Gus," she said, giving him another hug. "What would I do without you?"

"You'd have a decent job, instead of smelling like fish and wrestling with that damn boat every day. Not to mention you'd be sleeping in your own bed at night." He slapped his hand on the table. "That's what."

"Stop it, Gus. Thank God you were here when I needed you."

"You wouldn't have needed my help if I hadn't introduced you to that damn tourist."

"Thanks to that tourist, I have my own boat," she said lightly. "So I'm glad you introduced me to Kyle Franklin."

"You should have let me buy it," Gus muttered as he poured himself another cup of coffee. "This isn't a job for a woman."

"Geez, Gus, don't you ever quit?" Charlotte added milk to her own coffee and curled up on the bench. "Haven't we had this discussion about a million times? I *wanted* the boat. I'm not going to sell it to you."

"I could use another one," he said, fixing her with a defiant look. "I got more business than I can handle."

"Give it up," she said, shaking her head. "The

only thing you need less is another hole in that hard head of yours."

"I'm going to bug you until you say yes."

"I'm never going to say yes," she answered. "I'm a charter captain. What would I do without a boat? Let's talk about something else. Have you talked to Kat lately?"

Gus smiled. "She called last night. She said she was doing good, but she sounded tired. She's worried about Regan, and dollars to doughnuts she's working too hard at the clinic." He jerked his chin at Charlotte. "You're just like her. And that's scary."

"That's because you raised us right."

"You'd better not tell her I was down here," he muttered. "Her lectures are worse than her mother's." He shook his head. "Kat and that red hair of hers is scary when she gets in a temper."

"Don't worry. If you go home after you finish your coffee, I won't say a word."

"All right," he said, his face pale and his eyes weary. "But first tell me about this reporter."

"He's from Green Bay," she said airily. "He said he was writing a history of Sturgeon Falls. He wanted to talk to you since you're one of the oldest living residents."

Gus stood up. "You've got a smart mouth, Charlotte Burns."

"Gee," she said, "who do you think I got that from?"

Gus looked around the cabin one more time. "Thank you," he said quietly. "For taking care of the boat for me."

"Anytime," she said. "You know that, Gus."

"No more sleeping here."

"I wouldn't think of it," she answered.

He snorted and walked onto the deck, Charlotte following him. She knew he was seeing the missing fishing poles and cushions.

"You say this reporter showed up at the same time as the kids?" he asked. "Are you sure he was a reporter?"

"He showed me his ID from the newspaper. It looked authentic."

"IDs can be faked easier than spit. Maybe he was with the kids."

Charlotte frowned. "I don't think so. One of the kids hit him in the mouth. And he never said a word about the marina or buying out our leases." She felt her face turn pink. "I had dinner with him last night, and I don't think he knew about the developers until I told him."

"He's just trying to catch you off guard with an expensive, fancy dinner."

"Hardly fancy." She laughed. "We went to Nightingales. But I'll ask him next time I see him."

Gus frowned. "Next time? I thought he wanted to talk to me."

"I can tell him just as much about Sturgeon Falls as you can," she said, shrugging. "So I'll take care of it."

"You watch yourself with this slick city guy," Gus said darkly. "You can't trust any of them."

"Don't worry. I learned my lesson." She stepped onto the pier. "Come on. I'll walk you to your car."

"Making sure I leave?"

Charlotte kissed his cheek. "No, spending a couple of extra minutes with you. I don't get to do that often enough."

TWO DAYS LATER, Charlotte balanced a bundle of flowers on her hip and rang the doorbell of the Macauley home. As she leaned against the railing, she heard the crisp taps of someone's footsteps crossing the hardwood floor.

"Charlotte." Frances smiled as she opened the door. "Come in."

She enfolded Charlotte in a tight embrace. "How are you, sweetheart?"

"I'm good. How are you?" Charlotte touched the cast on the older woman's left arm.

"I'm doing just fine. You and Kat and Gus are spoiling me."

"That's because we love you. And you deserve to be spoiled." She handed Frances the flowers. "I thought you might like these."

Frances looked into the paper cone that held the mixture of roses, lilies and alstromeria. "They're beautiful. But how many times do I have to tell you not to spend your money on me?"

Charlotte kissed her cheek. "How many times do I have to tell you they don't cost me anything? The shop was going to throw them away because they're already at their peak. I rescued them from the landfill."

"Charlotte Burns, are you still working at that flower shop?" Cradling the bouquet in the curve of her cast, Frances put her right hand on her hip and tried to look stern. "As busy as you've been on the boat?"

"Only a couple of evenings a week," she answered breezily. "The extra money comes in handy. And since my bookings are filling up, this will be the last week."

"Maybe you should sell the boat."

"You're as bad as Gus." Charlotte took the flowers from Frances and headed toward the kitchen. "Let's put these in water."

"Don't try to change the subject on me," Frances warned from behind her. "Gus told me you were sleeping on his boat. You're going to make yourself sick."

"There hasn't been any more vandalism," Charlotte said, reaching into a cabinet and pulling down the crystal vase. "So it's worth it." She smiled as she filled the vase with water, sprinkled in the preservative, then arranged the flowers. "If nothing happens in the next couple of days, I'll go back to sleeping at home."

"I'm worried about you, Charlotte."

"I know you are. Do you have any idea how good that makes me feel?"

Smiling, Frances reached for the kettle. "You always did know how to stop me in my tracks when I was getting up a head of steam. Kat could take lessons from you." As she filled the kettle with water, she asked over her shoulder, "Can you stay for a bit? I'll make some tea."

"That sounds great."

After the water boiled, Charlotte carried their

mugs into the backyard and helped Frances settle in the glider. Taking a sip of tea, Frances asked, "Have you seen your mother lately?"

Charlotte gripped her mug more tightly. "I talked to her a few weeks ago," she said. "She found a job as a greeter at one of the discount stores in Green Bay."

"Wonderful." Frances patted Charlotte's hand. "You can stop worrying so much."

"It won't last long," Charlotte said, trying to keep the bitterness out of her voice.

"Now you don't know that," Frances objected. "Maybe she'll stick with it this time."

"Maybe." And maybe pigs would fly soon, too. "How's Gus doing?"

"Cantankerous as ever. But I think he's doing better."

"He wants to get back on his boat real bad."

"Thank you for dealing with the insurance and the police," Frances said, grasping her hand. "He didn't need that stress."

"I know. He didn't need the stress of talking to that reporter, either." As soon as the words were out of her mouth, she knew she'd made a mistake. But she never censored herself around Gus and Frances.

"What reporter?" Frances asked, puzzled.

"He's from Green Bay. He's writing a story about Sturgeon Falls and the cherry orchards."

"What?" Tea splashed onto her hand as she looked at Charlotte. "Why would he ask Gus about the orchards?"

Startled by Frances's sharp tone, Charlotte

blotted the tea on the older woman's cast. "Be careful," she said. "You don't want a burn just when you're ready to get this off."

"What did the reporter want?" Frances asked again.

Her insistence made Charlotte look more closely at Frances, who wouldn't meet the younger woman's gaze. "I'm not sure. His questions were kind of vague."

"Why does he want to talk to Gus?"

Charlotte set her mug on the ground, noticing as she did that Frances's knuckles were white. "He thought Gus used to work for Van Allen. I told him he was mistaken, and he hasn't been back since." Not that she was paying attention.

"He shouldn't be bothering you," Frances said fiercely.

"I didn't mind." Charlotte took her hand. "He's a good-looking guy who bought me dinner the other night. It was almost a date," she teased. "You've been pestering me to date more."

"I didn't think you'd take up with a reporter," Frances said, sniffing. "Especially one who's snooping around things that are none of his business."

Charlotte's smile faded. "What do you have against reporters?"

Frances extracted her hand from Charlotte's and looked away. "Nothing. I just don't want anyone taking advantage of you."

"*Taking advantage of me?* Don't you know me any better than that?" Charlotte studied Frances's profile. Her mouth was a thin, hard line.

Frances finally looked at her. "I guess I'm still trying to protect you. I forget that you and Kat are grown women."

"Hey, it's all right," Charlotte said, wrapping her arm around Frances, wondering about the shadows in the older woman's eyes. "I like the way you look out for me."

"You don't need me butting in," Frances said, rising from the glider. "Walk with me into the house. I've been selfish, keeping you here so long. I know you have a million things to do today." Her smile was forced. "I'll give you some chili you can heat up for dinner."

Charlotte stood, wondering why Frances was in a hurry to get rid of her all of a sudden. "You know I can't resist your chili." She opened the door to the kitchen. "I may be spoiling you now, but you've been spoiling me for years, Frances."

Frances's expression softened. "You're the daughter of my heart, Charlotte. You're the other child Gus and I wanted so badly."

And Frances and Gus were the parents she'd wanted so badly. "Right back at you," Charlotte said, kissing her on the cheek. "I'll see you soon."

CHAPTER FOUR

Two days later, as Charlotte pulled off County B into Kendall Van Allen's driveway, she could've kicked herself when she realized she was looking for Dylan's car. Kendall. She was here to see her friend.

Not Dylan Smith.

Dylan had said he'd call, and he hadn't. End of story. And it was just as well. She'd spent far too much time thinking about him in the past few days. He'd spent their evening together going out of his way to charm and entertain her, and that should have been a warning signal.

She had no intention of getting involved with another charmer.

She ignored the tiny jolt she felt when she saw Smith's car parked next to Kendall's house. Giving it a wide berth, she turned off the ignition, grabbed the newspaper-wrapped fish from the seat and jumped out.

Voices drifted down the stairs and, through the screen door, she saw the shadowy figures of a man and a woman separate. Kendall opened the door, her face flushed and her eyes bright. "Charlotte! Come on in."

As she stepped into the kitchen, Kendall took Gabe Townsend's hand. "You know Gabe, don't you?"

"We got reacquainted last time I was here," Charlotte said. "How are you, Gabe?"

"Couldn't be better," he said, bringing Kendall's hand to his mouth.

"Gabe and I are getting married," Kendall said, one arm around Gabe's waist.

"I'd heard that," Charlotte said. She hugged Kendall with her free arm. "Congratulations. I'm happy for both of you." And she was. She was thrilled her friend was so happy. But she couldn't help feeling a twinge of loneliness.

"You heard already?" Kendall shook her head. "Gabe just proposed last week. The gossip pipeline in Sturgeon Falls is so efficient it's frightening."

"It was your guest, Dylan Smith. He told me."

"Really?" Kendall's forehead furrowed. "I didn't know you knew Dylan."

"He came to the marina looking for Gus and found me instead. In fact, he helped me chase off a couple of kids vandalizing Gus's boat."

"What? What happened?"

Charlotte repeated the story. "Whatever the reason, they haven't been back."

"And Smith showed up just as you were chasing them off Gus's boat?" Gabe frowned. "That's convenient."

"Stop being so snarky about Dylan, Gabe. Why on earth would he trash Gus's boat?"

"Who knows why he does half the stuff he does?" Gabe muttered. But the tightness around his mouth disappeared as he bent to kiss Kendall.

Charlotte set her package on the table. "I hope you're not sick of fish. My charter this morning said, and I quote, 'Ewwww' when I offered them recipes for salmon."

"Thanks, Charlotte," Kendall said, handing her a glass of iced tea before sliding the catch into the refrigerator. "We always enjoy your fish."

"There will probably be more in the next few weeks. I'm helping Gus cover some of his booked groups."

"How's Gus doing?" Kendall asked.

"Better. But he's still forbidden to take out charters." Charlotte sighed. "It's killing him."

"I bet. What did he have to say to Dylan?"

"They haven't talked. I didn't want Gus bothered."

"Why was he looking for Gus, anyway?" Gabe asked.

Charlotte shrugged. "He didn't say, really. Just that he wanted to talk to him for a story he was doing about the orchard. I told him he'd gotten some wrong information. Gus never worked there." She sipped her iced tea and watched Kendall and Gabe exchange a look.

"What? Do you know what this is about?" she demanded.

Kendall glanced at Gabe. "Maybe. Dylan said he was here in Sturgeon Falls looking for his father. He'd heard he worked at the Van Allen orchard."

"His father?" Charlotte carefully set the glass on the counter. "He thinks Gus is his father?"

"We're guessing he thinks it was Stuart. You know that old hound dog couldn't keep his pants zipped. After Stuart died, Carter had to deal with a couple of women who claimed Stuart had fathered their kids. Thank God for DNA."

"So why would Dylan want to talk to Gus?"

"Who knows?" Kendall said. "Probably to see if Gus can tell him about Stuart, maybe find out if his mother had been involved with him. I think he's trying to get as many scraps of information as he can. He was talking to the mother of one of our workers, too."

"Good. Keep him talking to people at the orchard," Charlotte said. "Maybe he'll leave Gus alone."

"Wow." Kendall leaned against the granite counter and raised her eyebrows. "It looks like Dylan rubbed you the wrong way."

Charlotte sipped her iced tea. She had no intention of telling her friend she'd fallen for the old "I'll call you" routine. "He didn't make a big impression," she said, staring at her tea. "So tell me about the wedding."

"It's going to be next month. Just family and close friends." She took Charlotte's hand. "You'll be a bridesmaid, won't you?"

"Of course. Although I know that's just an excuse to get me into a frilly dress." She set her glass down and grimaced at Kendall.

"Nah. I was thinking more of a slinky dress." Kendall glanced down at Charlotte's boots. "And maybe some sexy sandals, too."

"They'd be wasted on the fish."

Kendall tugged on Charlotte's ponytail. "There's more to life than catching fish and getting up at ungodly hours of the morning to do it," she said. "You need to get a life, Charlotte."

"Been there, done that, got the T-shirt." She edged toward the door. She *so* did not want to run into Dylan, especially after this conversation. "Thanks for the tea, Kendall. And congratulations again, you two. You deserve every happiness."

"Thanks, Charlotte," Gabe said.

"Don't you have a company down in Milwaukee?" Charlotte suddenly asked him. "Are you going to commute?"

"My business is easy to move. And speaking of which, do you want me to take a look at the security setup on Gus's boat? And yours?"

"We don't have any security. We've never needed it. I've been sleeping on Gus's boat, and that seems to be doing the trick. But thanks for asking."

Gabe winked. "You and Gus will get the family discount."

Charlotte headed down the stairs as Kendall called, "Thanks again for the salmon."

Charlotte waved in her direction and kept going. She'd almost made it to her truck when she heard, "Charlotte?"

She turned around reluctantly. "Hey, Smith," she said as she opened her truck door. "How's it going?"

"Good. I'm glad to see you. Were you looking for me?"

"I was here to see Kendall. Why would I be looking for you?" she asked, managing to sound genuinely puzzled.

"I'm sorry. I said I'd call and I didn't. But stuff came up." He edged closer. "I wanted to call."

"Don't worry about it," Charlotte said. She was angry at herself for having wasted even one moment waiting for him to call. And the hurt that shimmered beneath the anger made her uneasy. "I haven't given you a thought."

"No?" His eyes twinkled. "I've thought about you. A lot."

"Save it, Smith. Don't waste my time. Or yours." She swung into the cab of her truck.

He put a hand on her door. "Wait a minute, Charlotte. I wasn't blowing you off."

"You think I'm sulking because I haven't heard from you?" She shook her head. "Get over yourself. I don't sulk."

His gaze traveled over her face, then dipped down to her chest, and her nipples tightened. "No, Charlotte, I don't imagine you do. That wrench of yours is more your style."

She resisted the impulse to cross her arms over her chest. "What's your point?"

His slow smile made her toes curl. "I'm willing to risk the wrench. I can move real fast."

"Tell me something I don't know," she muttered.

"Can you stay for a few minutes? There's someone I'd like you to meet."

Charlotte thought of the groceries she needed to

buy, the deck that needed to be scrubbed and the lures she wanted to tie. Curiosity trumped errands every time.

"I suppose I can give you a few minutes," she said, opening her door and climbing out.

"Great." He grabbed her hand, but she snatched it away from him.

He grinned. "Starting at square one again, are we?"

"I don't believe we got past square one," she shot back.

He put his hand over his heart. "I love it when you talk mean to me."

In spite of herself, she laughed. And that made her even more uneasy. "I definitely need a weapon when I deal with you."

He stopped walking. "That's a completely different ball game. If you had a weapon, I'd have to take it away from you." He leaned in. "That would involve bodily contact."

When she realized she was swaying closer to him, Charlotte moved away. Dylan hesitated, then he indicated a group of girls playing soccer in the field in front of the orchard.

Charlotte recognized Kendall's daughters, Shelby and Jenna, but the other two were strangers. One had a long, dark braid and looked about the same age as Shelby. The other, tall with shaggy, dark red hair, appeared older.

"Hayley," Dylan called, and the older girl stopped in her tracks. "Come here for a moment."

Shelby and Jenna saw Charlotte and ran over.

"Charlotte!" they both yelled, almost knocking her over in their enthusiasm.

"Hey, guys." Charlotte draped an arm over their shoulders. "What's going on?"

"We're practicing for my soccer tournament," Shelby said. "My friend Elena—" she pointed to the girl with the long braid "—and Hayley are helping." She glanced at her younger sister. "And Jenna, too," she added quickly.

"Good luck. I wish I could see you play."

"We might have another tournament after the fishing season," Shelby said.

"I'll be there if you do." She watched as Shelby and Jenna ran toward Elena. Then she turned to Dylan. He had his arm around the other girl, who was staring at Charlotte.

"You having fun?" Dylan was asking her.

The girl nodded. "Yeah. Shelby's pretty good, and so is Elena." The other three had resumed playing. "Jenna's lame, but she's just a kid."

Charlotte hid a smile as Dylan laughed. "Yeah, she's four whole years younger than you."

He swung Hayley around to face Charlotte. "Ms. Burns, I'd like you to meet my daughter, Hayley."

Stunned, Charlotte responded automatically when the girl shook her hand. "Hi, Hayley. It's very nice to meet you. Please, call me Charlotte."

"Okay." Hayley studied Charlotte speculatively. "Are you my dad's girlfriend?"

"No!" Charlotte said, too quickly. "We, uh, met because he needs to talk to me for a story he's doing."

"Cool. Can I go back to the game now?"

"Sure," Dylan said, ruffling her hair. "Just don't beat them too badly."

Hayley's grin was a mirror of her father's. "I'm going to kick their butts."

Charlotte's throat tightened as she watched the love and understanding between Dylan and his daughter, and she took a step back. She wasn't part of that circle of two.

Then Hayley ran off, calling over her shoulder, "Nice to meet you, Charlotte!"

"Nice to meet you, too." But she wasn't sure Hayley heard her. The girl had kicked the soccer ball into play and run after it, leaving the other three scrambling to catch up.

"That's why I haven't called you," Dylan said. "Hayley's been here for the past few days."

My God. Was he married? "How about Hayley's mother?" she asked, feeling sick. "Is she here, too?"

"We're divorced," he answered, frowning. "Do you think I would have asked you out if I was married?"

"You wouldn't be the first."

"You told me you don't cheat. Neither do I. Hayley's mother and I have been divorced for ten years."

"Good," she said without thinking. "I mean…it's good to know I wasn't poaching the other night."

"Not at all."

Hayley was laughing at something Shelby had said over in the grass. "You have a daughter," she said, trying to adjust her image of Dylan.

"Yeah. She's my world."

"She has very good manners. She seems like a nice kid," Charlotte said.

"She's hell on wheels," Dylan said. "In the nicest possible way."

"I never pictured you as a father."

"I have hidden depths."

"Apparently so. Are you able to spend a lot of time with Hayley?"

"I have an apartment that's close to her mother's house," he said. "So Hayley sees a lot of both of us. Except when I'm on the road, working on a story. I don't like to be away. I call her every night when I'm gone."

She shoved her hands into her pockets. "If it's so hard to be away from Hayley, what are you doing here? You say you're working on a story about the orchard, but no one's interested in what happened here years ago. It's just a business, boring and pre-dictable. Even Kendall, who loves the orchard, would tell you that. Who's going to want to read a story about the history of a cherry orchard?"

He stared past her at Hayley and the other girls. "I'm not writing about trees," he said, a hint of impa-tience in his voice. "I'm writing about the people who've worked with the trees. A lot of men and women have come and gone in this orchard over the years, and every one of them has a story." Suddenly he seemed very old. "I want to know about the people."

"Why?"

"People are endlessly fascinating." He shrugged

without looking at her. "Call it my reporter's curiosity."

So he wasn't going to tell her why he was here—if he'd told Kendall and Gabe the truth about searching for his father. "Seems like there are a lot of other stories more interesting than a cherry orchard."

"Like what's going on at the marina?" She watched him struggle to lighten the mood. "Do you think I should write about that, Charlotte?"

She ran her hand over the rough bark of a cherry tree. "I'm not going to tell you what to do. I think you should write what you want to write."

"How about a deal? You put me in touch with Gus Macauley and I'll get started on that story about your marina. That will bring attention to what's going on."

"You think so? You're not very humble, are you, Smith?"

"I told you the other day I don't do humble. I'm just telling you the way it is."

"Is that right?" Anger built in her, and she welcomed it. "You think I'd let you harass my friend for some free publicity?"

"*Harass?* For God's sake, Charlotte. I just want to talk to him." He shook his head. "You're mad at me because I didn't call, and you're punishing me by keeping me away from Gus."

"What?" Her fear that it was true only fueled her anger. "For crying out loud, Smith. We had dinner, not a lifelong commitment. You think I'm that pathetic and needy?"

He snorted. "You're the least needy woman I've ever met. But you're taking this protecting Gus too far. I want to know why."

"Gus has been sick," she said without thinking. "He's not up to being interviewed right now. Okay? I'm not trying to punish you. I don't care that you didn't call me."

"Liar," he said softly.

"You can go to hell," she retorted. "And you can take your story about the marina with you. I didn't realize it was payback for access to Gus. It would upset him if he knew that. Gus doesn't care much for people who can be bought."

She pushed away from the tree. "Someone who's for sale shouldn't be writing about the marina, anyway. Credibility, you know?"

She was surprised to read hurt beneath his anger. "Fine. Write your own damn story. And good luck getting it into your local paper."

"Goodbye, Smith," she said, holding his gaze for a beat longer than necessary. She didn't offer to shake his hand.

He didn't look away. "So long, Charlotte."

She stepped out of the shade of the cherry trees and headed toward her car. "It was nice meeting your daughter," she added over her shoulder. "She seems like a nice kid. She must take after her mother."

It was a cheap shot. But it felt very good.

CHAPTER FIVE

DYLAN WALKED DOWN the pier to Charlotte's boat, slowing when he passed Macauley's slip. No signs of life. Charlotte had said Gus would be back in a week, but Dylan couldn't wait that long. His vacation time was running out.

Most of the other boats were gone, and those still docked were closed and silent. It was what he'd expected—at ten in the morning in June, most captains would be out. The deserted marina was almost eerily silent. The only sounds he heard were the cries of the gulls and the slapping of the waves against the pier pilings.

Charlotte's slip was empty. He'd talked to several of the captains, and realized there was a rhythm to their work. They took a charter out early in the morning and another in the late afternoon. Occasionally they were lucky enough to get another trip in the middle of the day.

He sat down and rested his back against the weathered wood of one of the posts. He was engrossed in his notes, adding observations and questions he wanted to ask, when he heard the rumble of an engine.

He could tell from a distance that it was Charlotte's boat. The splash of orange and pink from the flower boxes made the *Water Lily* stand out. He waited until it was close to the dock, then he stood.

Charlotte jumped out and tied the boat, then stepped back onto the deck. The four men with her didn't look like they were in a hurry to leave. Sunburned and holding beers, they stood too close to Charlotte, talking and laughing. And Charlotte was laughing right back.

She eased away from them and perched on the railing. One of the men gestured toward the parking lot, and Dylan could read his body language as easily as if he'd heard the man.

They wanted Charlotte to join them. Off the boat.

She smiled and shook her head, still apparently at ease and friendly, but Dylan saw a hint of wariness in the rigidity of her shoulders. When one of the men took a step toward her, Dylan sprang onto the deck.

"Hey, honey, how was the trip?" he said, brushing a kiss over her cheek. "You're back early. Did someone get seasick?" he asked, smiling politely.

The closest man stared at Dylan for a long second. "Nah," he finally said. "We all got a salmon, so we decided to quit while we were ahead."

"Charlotte knows where to find them," Dylan said. "She's the best." He read irritation in Charlotte's expression. "Don't forget her when you want to book another trip."

"We won't," the first man said, letting his gaze

linger on Charlotte longer than necessary. Then he got off the boat, followed by the rest of the men. They said goodbye, but their smiles were gone. Dylan heard the *clink* of glass and realized they'd dumped the beers in a trash can.

Charlotte watched them leave with a mixture of relief and irritation. When they disappeared from view, she stood up. "What was that all about?"

Dylan shrugged. "They didn't seem to want to leave. So I helped them along."

She glanced toward the parking lot again as she wiped her damp hands on her jeans. "Those men were customers, Smith." Customers who had creeped her out. "My customers spend a lot of money on their charters. If they want to stick around and talk for a few minutes afterward, I'm happy to humor them."

"Those guys didn't want to talk," he said quietly. "They wanted you to go somewhere with them. Didn't they?"

She brushed past him and picked up a hose hanging over the railing, disgusted when she saw her hand tremble. She sprayed the deck down, then grabbed a rag and scrubbed furiously, trying to still the adrenaline churning through her veins. When every inch of the deck was dry, she tossed the rag into a corner.

"Yes," she finally said. She took a deep breath to steady herself. She should be angry with Dylan for interfering. Not grateful. "They wanted me to have a drink with them."

"And they didn't like hearing no," Dylan said.

"No one likes hearing no. But I would have handled them." She grabbed a fishing pole and fiddled with the sinker. "You were out of line, acting like a caveman." Her fingers moved expertly along the fiberglass, adjusting the green-and-blue lure. "I would have made sure they left with a smile. I don't want my customers to go away unhappy."

"They'll get over it."

"But I won't get their business again."

"No big loss," Dylan said.

"No big loss?" Charlotte carefully set the pole down. "I have five months to make my living with this boat," she said. "I only get paid when I book a charter. And part of my job is to make nice with the customers. Talk to them. Laugh at their jokes. Make them feel as if they're the most important people in the world."

She wiped her hands on her jeans. "And you know what? For the three or four or five hours that they're on my boat, they *are* the most important people in the world. I build my business through repeat customers and referrals. Those men aren't going to refer anyone to me."

"That's good," he said, watching her pace. "There was something off about those guys."

"And you know this from your extensive experience on fishing charters?"

He shrugged. "I'm a reporter. I can read people. I didn't like the vibe from them."

"They'd all had a couple of beers. That was the only *vibe* you were getting."

"There's no one around right now," he said, waving his hand. "The marina is deserted. There were four of them, Charlotte. And there's one of you."

A young man with light blond hair stuck his nose out of the cabin. "Everything okay, Charlotte?"

"Everything's fine. Our customers left without their fish." She nodded toward the cooler. "Go ahead and fillet them, then put them on ice. They'll probably be back later to pick them up."

"Gotcha." The guy wrestled the cooler onto the dock, then picked it up and headed toward the marina.

Dylan stared after the man until he was out of sight. "Sorry," he said stiffly. "I was out of line."

"Knock it off with the testosterone," she said. "That was my first mate, Steve. He's a twenty-two-year-old kid."

His face relaxed. "Okay, so you weren't alone. But that doesn't change the fact that those four guys didn't look like they'd take no for an answer."

"Oh, for God's sake. Are you sure you don't write fiction? You've got a real talent for melodrama. They were harmless."

"Are you sure?" He took a step closer. He smelled like fresh air. "Are you completely sure they were harmless?"

No. "Back off, Smith. I can take care of myself. I don't need anyone running interference for me." She swiped at a tendril of hair that had come loose from her ponytail. "Sticking his nose where it doesn't belong."

Dylan held up his hands. "Fine. Sorry I drove

your customers away. I'll keep my opinions to myself next time."

"There won't be a next time," she said. "We were finished a couple of days ago. What are you doing here?"

"I came to apologize," he said, keeping his eyes on hers. "For what happened the other day. I shouldn't have joked about trading an interview with Gus for the story about the marina. I shouldn't have said you were punishing me because I didn't call. My only excuse is that I was frustrated." He touched her cheek. "In a lot of ways."

She batted his hand away. "Fine. Apology accepted. Now go away."

He didn't move. "I started the story about the marina."

"You did?" She studied him, not sure whether to believe him.

"Yep. I've already talked to several of the captains." He named a few, and she was impressed. He'd gotten interviews with men on both sides of the issue.

She wiped another spot on the rail, not looking at him. "Why are you doing this, Smith?"

"It's a story that interested me." He paused. "But I'm writing it because I told you I would."

"A man of your word?"

"Absolutely." He tucked the notebook into his shirt pocket. "It's the only thing I have to offer most of my sources—that I'll do what I say I'll do. And that I won't reveal who they are. Under any circumstances."

"You just told me who you interviewed for your story," she pointed out.

"They gave me permission to use their names. The rest didn't."

Charlotte sighed as she sat on the step up to the cabin. "All right, Smith. I accept your apology."

"You already said that."

She smiled. "I didn't mean it before."

"So we're square?"

"We're square." She patted the step next to her, and he sat down.

"Tell me the truth, Charlotte. Didn't those guys make you just a little nervous?"

She stared across the water, remembering the hair rising on the back of her neck whenever one of them got too close. "Yes, they made me nervous. All right? Are you happy?"

"How did they make you nervous?"

"They didn't seem like they were really into fishing. They weren't interested." They were more interested in *her*—they had invaded her personal space too many times for it to be accidental.

"Don't you get a lot of people who aren't really fishermen? People who want to try a fishing charter?"

"Of course. But they're usually enthusiastic. They ask questions. And they almost always have a good time and get excited about catching fish. Especially when they're big salmon like those guys caught this morning."

"And they didn't get excited?"

"Nope. They acted as if catching a fish was their job. Not something they were doing for fun. And they didn't even want to try to catch their limit."

Dylan pulled out his notebook and began to write. Charlotte leaned forward, but he turned so she couldn't see.

"What are you writing?"

"A description of them," he said, adding a few more notes and then closing the book and putting it back in his pocket. "In case they decide to come back and persuade you to go for that drink."

"They're not coming back," she said. "Trust me."

"You never know." He folded his arms across his chest. "Maybe they picked you deliberately. Maybe they weren't here for the fishing. Maybe they work for the developer and they wanted to convince you to get Gus to change his mind."

"You weren't kidding, were you? You like conspiracy theories."

"The lifeblood of an investigative reporter," he said lightly.

"I won't take them out again. Satisfied?"

His gaze felt like a caress on her hair, her flannel shirt, her worn jeans. "No. I'm not."

Her cheeks heated as she moved away from him and picked up another fishing rod. The flasher caught the sun and reflected into her eyes, blinding her and preventing her from seeing him as she tied on a new lure. "Too bad. That's as far as I'm willing to go."

"Is it, Charlotte?"

Her hands slipped on the lure and the barb pricked

her thumb. "What do you expect me to do?" she asked, sucking on the bead of blood. "Put out a hit on them?"

Dylan laughed softly. "That's good. You think on your feet. I like a challenge."

She felt his eyes on her. "So are we done, Smith? You came to apologize, I accepted, and now you'll let me get back to work?"

"Do you have another charter this afternoon?"

"Yes." She set the rod on the floor. "I'm taking a group out for Gus."

"How is Gus doing, by the way?"

"Better." But still not back to his old self. And she was worried.

"I heard his pneumonia was pretty serious."

She swung around to face him. "How do you know that?"

"How do you think? I asked some questions, talked to some people."

"I told you he was sick. Didn't you believe me?"

"Doesn't matter. You know what they tell journalists—if your mom says she loves you, check it out."

"Why is it so important to talk to Gus?" Frances's reaction to questions about the orchard lingered in Charlotte's mind. Digging into the orchard would upset the woman. And that would upset Gus.

"He worked there. I have questions only an employee could answer."

"I'm sure he'll talk to you when he's better." She'd make sure Frances wasn't around when he did.

He shoved his hand through his hair. "I don't

have much time left," he said. "I can't twiddle my thumbs for a week."

"I'm sorry, but Gus doesn't need any extra stress right now."

"And you find me stressful?"

God help her, she did. "We're not talking about me."

He smiled. "That's good. I wouldn't want you to think I'm an impetuous guy. I can be very patient, Charlotte. I know how to take it slow." He lowered his voice. "There are times when I'm a big fan of slow."

He smoothed his knuckles across her cheek, and she felt a sizzle down to her toes. She pushed his hand away, but it was too late. She wanted to feel that sizzle again.

Dylan shoved his hands into his pockets. "Are you going to be out late again tonight?"

"Why do you ask?"

"I was hoping you'd go out with me."

"Sorry," she said, and realized she meant it. "I have plans tonight." She wanted to see Gus and Frances, and they would be at the VFW fish boil.

"Too bad. There's a fish boil at the VFW. I wanted you to go with me and Hayley."

He was going to the fish boil? She stared at him. "Why do you want to do that? Fish boils are for tourists." It was the first thing that came to her mind.

"Really? I've been told that this fish boil is the best place to talk to the Sturgeon Falls old-timers. It's strictly locals."

"So you're going to show up and start interviewing?"

"Of course not. That would be rude. I just want to meet people. And this sounds like a great opportunity. But if you can't make it, don't worry. Hayley and I will go by ourselves."

He'd meet a lot of people at the VFW fish boil, she thought grimly. Including Gus and Frances. What would happen if Dylan asked questions about the orchard in front of Frances? "All right. How about you meet me here at nine o'clock?"

He shook his head. "That's way too late," he said. "I heard seven was the time to show up. If you're going to be out with a charter, you could meet me there later."

"I should be back by seven. But I wouldn't have time to change my clothes." She would, but it was the only excuse she could think of.

"Not a problem. I've been told it's casual."

"Fine. I'll meet you here at seven tonight."

"Great. Can we consider this our second date?"

"Our second date? As far as I'm concerned, we're starting over."

"Really?" His eyes twinkled, and she had the uneasy feeling that he'd seen all the way through her. "That's too bad."

"Why is that too bad?" She knew he was setting her up, but was too curious to resist.

"Because I have a strict rule about not kissing until the second date."

"Kissing? Who said there was going to be kissing?" Her voice sounded breathy and weak.

"Oh, there's going to be kissing, Charlotte. There's no doubt about that. I'm just giving you time to catch up."

He flashed her a grin as he jumped off the boat and disappeared down the pier.

CHAPTER SIX

CHARLOTTE WAS LOCKING UP the boat when she heard footsteps on the pier. Dylan. It was pathetic that she recognized his footsteps.

"Hey, Charlotte. You look good." He spoke softly. "I thought you wouldn't have time to change."

Self-conscious, she brushed her hands over the flowery skirt. Kat had insisted she buy it last time they went shopping. For hot dates, she'd teased. "We got in earlier than I expected."

His gaze skimmed her hair and she felt a flicker of heat. "And you left your hair down, too."

She shrugged and felt the unfamiliar ripple of curls across her shoulders. "It's something different."

"Different can be good."

There was an undercurrent in Dylan's voice that made her tingle with anticipation. "Hi, Hayley," she said quickly when she belatedly saw his daughter standing next to him.

"Is this your boat?" the girl asked, tucking a strand of auburn hair behind her ear. "The one you take out on fishing trips?"

"It is. Would you like a tour?"

"Yeah!" The girl's face lit up. "I've never been on a boat like this before. Why does it say *Water Lily* on the back of your boat?" she asked as she scrambled over the railing.

"The *Water Lily* is her name." Charlotte saw Dylan glance at his watch and smothered a smile. "Do you want to see the inside and go down to the galley?"

"Sure. What's a galley?"

"It's a kitchen on a boat. But there's more down there than a kitchen." Charlotte unlocked the door to the cabin and stepped inside.

"You have a couch? On a boat?" Hayley sat on the battered plaid sofa and bounced a couple of times. "That's cool."

"My customers need a comfortable place to sit when they're not fishing," Charlotte answered. She nodded at the pilot's seat. "That's where I steer the boat."

Hayley bounded up and climbed into the chair. "Is it like driving a car?"

"A little bit." Charlotte watched with a smile, entranced by Hayley's enthusiasm. It reminded her of herself at that age.

Pushing away from the wall and heading for the stairs, she said, "The galley is down here. Be careful, though. It's steep."

Hayley descended carefully and her eyes widened as she saw the table in the corner with the bench on two sides, the tiny refrigerator and stove. "It looks just like a real kitchen."

"That's because it is. You can live on a boat like this, if you wanted to."

"Can you sleep here?"

"Sure." Charlotte pointed toward the triangular room in the bow. "There are four bunks in there."

Hayley stuck her head in the dark room. "Cool!"

"Go ahead and try one."

Hayley clambered onto the thin mattress and lay down. "It's comfortable." She rolled over and peered out the porthole. "Can I sleep on your boat sometime?"

"Maybe." Charlotte glanced at Dylan. "I don't stay here very often."

Dylan had descended into the galley, and Charlotte wondered what he thought of the slightly shabby decor. The cushions on the benches around the table were worn and faded, the paneling chipped.

She didn't care. As long as the engine ran smoothly, she wasn't going to worry about the frayed cushions. Customers were hardly ever in the galley, anyway.

Dylan stepped closer, peering over her shoulder at Hayley. The girl was trying out all of the bunks, bouncing from one to the next. "Looks like you have yourself a convert," he said.

"It's fun to see how excited she is." Dylan was so near that the fresh, musky scent of his aftershave shimmered around her, and his breath stirred the hair above her ear. She felt hot, and she told herself it was because it was so warm inside the boat.

He raised his hand to look at his watch again and

pressed forward until his chest touched her back. Charlotte felt him all the way down to her toes, then he moved away as if the contact had been accidental.

"We should get going, Hayley," he said. "We don't want to miss the fish boil."

"In a minute. I have to close this window I opened. Fish boil sounds gross, anyway." The scorn in her voice was classic preteen. "I don't know why we're going."

"Why *are* you going, Dylan?" Charlotte murmured. She squeezed past in the narrow hallway, brushing against him. Two could play this game.

He tensed. "Why am I going where?"

"Why are you going to a gross fish boil?" She watched him struggle against reaching out to her.

"I don't know. It seems like a bad idea right now."

"Yeah?" She edged closer. "Why is that?"

"Take a guess, Charlotte." He skimmed a finger down her cheek, down her neck, hooking it in the collar of her blouse. His knuckle scraped her collarbone and her pulse leaped. "Or do I have to explain in more detail?"

"Details are always good." Her voice sounded breathless and thin.

"Later," he murmured. "I'll give you all the details you want."

"What's this door?" Hayley's voice came from behind Charlotte. Right behind her. Swallowing, she turned around and tried to focus. "That door? That's the head."

"What's the head?"

"It's a bathroom." Charlotte opened the door and Hayley peered inside.

"Wow. The sink is so tiny. And so is the toilet." She stuck her head around the door. "It even has a shower." Hayley spun around. "Dad, did you know you could take a shower on a boat?"

"Let's see." Dylan trapped Charlotte between his body and the wall, draping one arm casually across her shoulders, and stuck his head in the room. Out of Hayley's sight, hidden in the shadows, he let his hand drop across Charlotte's breast. Once, then again.

"That's a tiny shower," he said, cupping her breast in his palm, then easing away from her. His hand trailed over her hair, tangling in her curls. "It would be a tight squeeze."

"Have you taken showers here?" Hayley asked.

"I have," Charlotte managed to say. "I took a shower tonight, right before you got here."

"I'd like to do that sometime," Hayley said.

"Me, too," Dylan added, his voice a slide of silk over her nerves.

Charlotte shivered as she walked up the stairs to the main cabin, aware of Dylan's gaze on her.

"We should go if you want to make the fish boil," Charlotte said. She had no experience with the sensual game she and Dylan were playing, and it had rattled her—enough to make her want to go to the fish boil. And the crowds that would be there.

Dylan waited for Hayley to jump onto the pier.

"What's the matter, Charlotte?" he murmured into her ear. "Start something you couldn't finish?"

"What are you talking about?" she answered, widening her eyes. "I thought you wanted to go to the VFW."

"Maybe not so much anymore."

"Fine. I can recommend some restaurants you and Hayley might enjoy." And she could escape onto her boat, alone, where she knew who she was.

"That's not how it works, Burns." He helped her onto the pier, smoothing his thumb over the back of her hand. "When you start something, you need to finish it."

"I didn't start a thing," she said.

"No?" He raised his eyebrows as he stepped out beside her. "Maybe we'll discuss that later."

ONCE THEY GOT into Dylan's car, Hayley stuck white iPod earbuds into her ears. As she bopped to her own music in the backseat, Dylan looked at Charlotte. "You don't want me at this fish boil. How come?" His voice was soft enough that Hayley wouldn't be able to hear over her music.

"I never said that."

"You didn't have to," he said drily. "Let's just say your actions spoke louder than words."

"I'll know a lot of people there."

"You don't want to be seen with me?"

"No!" She reached for his hand, drawing back at the last moment. "That's not it at all."

"Then why?"

"Because Gus and Frances will probably be there," she said after a long pause. He'd figure it out for himself soon enough.

"And you don't want me to meet Gus."

"Not in such a public place."

"You think I'm going to pepper him with questions in front of a crowd?"

It wasn't the crowd she was worried about. It was Frances. "It would be awkward."

"Charlotte, I've been doing this for over ten years. I know how to conduct an interview. And social occasions are not the place to do it. Okay?"

"Sorry," she said. "I didn't mean to insult you."

"You didn't."

"Maybe I'm too protective," she said, staring out the window into the gathering dusk. "But Gus is…excitable. And I don't want him to get worked up."

"Would questions about the orchard upset him?"

"Who knows?" She shook her head. But she knew questions about the orchard would upset Frances. She didn't want that to happen in a public place.

"Trust me, Charlotte. I'll be on my best behavior," he promised.

"Like you were on my boat?"

"No, that wasn't my best behavior. You're going to have to wait until later for my best."

She'd set herself up for that, she realized as he swung into the parking lot of the VFW.

Hayley leaned forward and pulled out the earbuds. "That looks cool," she said.

Glowing lights, strung between the trees, illuminated the grassy area behind the VFW hall. The big cast-iron kettle was set up on the asphalt, and Charlotte could see the steam pouring out of it. One of the VFW members stood at a table next to the kettle, serving up food. The picnic tables were almost filled, and a number of people stood on the grass, holding plates and talking.

As they got out, Hayley looked around. "This is all old people. You told me there'd be kids here."

"There'll be other kids here," Charlotte said.

"Let's get some food," Dylan said, steering her toward the crowd. "Are you hungry?"

Hayley looked skeptically at the plates people held, piled with fish and vegetables.

"Some people say that the boiled whitefish tastes like lobster," Charlotte said.

"Yeah?" Hayley perked up. "I had lobster once. I liked it."

"Then you'll probably like this."

"What do you want, Charlotte?" Dylan asked, standing in front of the man serving.

"Everything but the carrots," she replied absently, greeting an older couple who were friends of Gus and Frances. "Just tell Johnny it's for me. He knows what I want."

A few minutes later, Dylan handed her and Hayley plates of fish, corn and potatoes. She nodded toward an empty picnic table underneath the lanterns. "Do you want to sit there?"

"Looks good."

Hayley chattered to Dylan while they ate, telling him about swimming with Kendall's daughters that afternoon, then playing tag in the orchard. The bond between the pair was obvious, from the adoration in Hayley's eyes to the questions Dylan asked her. Questions that showed how interested he was in his daughter, in what she did and what she thought.

Charlotte envied them.

"Hey, Charlotte."

Charlotte jumped up. "Kat! How are you?"

Charlotte embraced her best friend, holding her tightly for a moment.

"I'm fine," Kat said in her low, husky voice. "How about you? I'm so glad you could make it tonight."

"I'm great." Charlotte squatted down to the child holding Kat's hand, who watched Charlotte with dark, hard-to-read eyes. "Hi, Regan. How are you doing?"

"Okay," the child said cautiously.

"How is soccer?" Charlotte asked.

The girl brightened. "I have a game tomorrow."

"Yeah? Maybe I'll stop by if I can."

Charlotte felt Dylan's gaze on her, and she reluctantly turned to him. "Kat, this is Dylan Smith. Dylan, this is my friend, Kat Macauley."

"Hi," Kat said, reaching out to shake his hand. "And this is Regan."

"Very nice to meet you, Kat." He shot a look at Charlotte she couldn't decipher. "And you, too, Regan. This is my daughter, Hayley."

Charlotte saw the interest in Regan's eyes as she looked at Hayley. Then the child moved closer to Kat.

"Do you need a place to sit?" Dylan asked, indicating the plate Kat held. "We can make room for you."

"Thanks." Kat and Regan slid onto the bench, and the child immediately bent to her food.

"You must be Gus Macauley's daughter," Dylan said.

"I am. Do you know Gus?"

"I haven't had the pleasure," Dylan said easily. "I understand he's been sick."

Kat sighed. "He was. And he's the world's worst patient—I'll never live him down."

"You're a doctor?" Dylan asked, then listened to Kat talk about her job and the clinic where she worked, asking questions, drawing her out.

Dylan was good, Charlotte had to admit. He focused on Kat as if there was no one else sitting at the table. That attention was hard to resist. Kat was already talking to Dylan as if she'd known him her whole life. Charlotte picked at her food, alternately impressed by Dylan's skill and irritated with Kat for succumbing so easily.

Finally, Regan interrupted. "I have to go to the bathroom," she said in a low voice.

"Okay." Kat and Hayley stood at the same time. "I can take her to the washroom," the girl said. "I was going anyway."

Kat looked uncertainly at Hayley, and Dylan smiled. "Hayley does a lot of babysitting," he assured Kat. "But I certainly understand if you don't want your daughter to go off with a stranger."

"Regan, do you want to go with Hayley, or do you want me to take you?" Kat asked, her hand resting softly on the child's shoulder.

"Hayley," Regan said.

"Okay."

Hayley carefully held Regan's hand as they walked away. "Wow," Charlotte said.

Kat watched them go. "She's getting a lot more adventurous."

"Regan usually sticks close to Kat," Charlotte told Dylan. She didn't want to explain about Regan or go into the details of their relationship. That would be like welcoming him to the Macauley family circle. And that was way too personal. Too intimate.

"Hayley is great with younger kids," Dylan said. "She's only twelve, but she does a lot of babysitting. The kid has more money than I do."

Keeping an eye on the toilets, Kat asked Charlotte, "Have you seen Mom and Dad?"

"Not for a couple of days." Charlotte knew Kat was asking if she'd seen them tonight. "How's Gus doing?"

"Go see for yourself." Kat nodded toward a knot of people standing on the grass. "They're right over there."

Charlotte clenched her hands in her lap, then carefully relaxed them. "Okay. I'll be right back, Dylan."

"Take your time. Hayley and I will find you."

Charlotte could feel Dylan's gaze on her back as she slipped through the crowd. She'd say a quick hello to Gus and Frances, then wander away before Dylan could find them.

"Hi, Frances." Charlotte kissed the older woman's cheek, and Frances beamed at her.

"Charlotte! I'm so glad you're here. I was hoping we'd have a chance to catch up."

"I, uh, brought someone," she muttered. "He wanted to see a fish boil."

"You brought a date?" Frances appeared both astonished and pleased.

"No, he's just a friend," Charlotte said firmly, giving Gus a hug. "How are you feeling?"

"Nothing wrong with me." He shot Frances a defiant look. "In fact, I'm going to take out a charter in the next couple of days."

"He's doing no such thing!" Frances said. "The doctor said a week, and it will be a week."

"See what I have to put up with?" Gus drank a gulp of beer and scowled. "She keeps me locked up like a dog."

Charlotte stifled a laugh. "I think you're exaggerating just a bit," she said. "I don't see a collar on you."

"She would if she thought she could get away with it," Gus grumbled.

"She's the love of your life, and you know it."

Gus looked at Frances, his expression softening. "I guess she does take pretty good care of me."

Frances tucked her arm through his. "I want you around for a few more years," she said. "I have plans for you."

"Yeah?" Gus winked at her. "What kind of plans?"

In the dim light, it looked as if Frances blushed. "Don't get smart with me, Gus Macauley."

The smile they shared was full of secrets, and loneliness crashed over Charlotte. What would it be like to have another person know her so intimately? Someone who would know what she was thinking with one glance?

She had no idea. She'd never had that kind of relationship. Not with her mother, and definitely not with her husband during their brief marriage.

She turned, unwilling to intrude on Gus and Frances's private moment, and bumped into Dylan. Hayley stood next to him, clearly bored.

"Hey," Dylan said, "are you going to introduce me to your friends?"

Charlotte sighed, silently acknowledging his tactics. If she refused, she'd be making a scene. Exactly what she'd told him she didn't want.

"Gus, Frances, this is Dylan Smith," she said, trying not to grit her teeth. "He's a reporter from Green Bay. And this is his daughter, Hayley. Dylan, Gus and Frances Macauley."

"Nice to meet you," Dylan said, shaking hands with them. "I'm enjoying your fish boil."

Frances touched his hand, then gave Charlotte a hard look. "*This* is your friend? The reporter?"

"Yes," Charlotte said, seeing the inexplicable

storm in Frances's eyes. "He wanted some of the local color, so I brought him here."

"We don't get many tourists at the VFW," Gus said.

"This fish boil is for locals," Frances said. The message was crystal clear. Dylan was an intruder.

"I don't consider myself a tourist," Dylan answered pleasantly. "Green Bay isn't that far."

"What kind of story are you writing?" Gus asked, sipping his beer.

"I'm not at the writing part yet," Dylan said. "I'm getting to know Sturgeon Falls and the cherry orchards."

"Good luck with your story, Mr. Smith," Frances said. Her voice had a cold edge that surprised Charlotte. The older woman clamped a hand on Gus's arm. "You'll have to excuse us. We should get going. Kat needs to get Regan to bed."

Her smile was forced. "We drove together so we'd have a chance to visit with Kat."

"I'll come say goodbye."

By the time she'd walked the four to their car, Dylan had wandered off. She finally found him talking to Jimmy Lane, the editor of the *Sturgeon Falls Herald*.

"Send me your story and I'll take a look at it," Jimmy said as Charlotte walked up. Hayley was kicking at a stone on the asphalt.

"Will do." Dylan shook hands with the other man, then turned to her. "I didn't mean to drive the Macauleys away."

"I think Frances was ready to leave," she said. Was it the orchard that upset Frances? It had to be—she'd had the same reaction last time Charlotte mentioned it. "Gus looked tired and Regan needed to get home."

"Thank you for introducing me," Dylan said as he steered Hayley toward the car.

"You were going to meet him eventually. I'm not trying to hide him from you," Charlotte muttered, winding her way through the parking lot.

"Could have fooled me."

When they exited the VFW parking lot, Dylan turned right instead of left. "Wrong way, Smith," she said.

"I'm driving Hayley to Van Allen House before I take you home," he said easily. "It's past her bedtime."

"Da-a-ad," Hayley said from the backseat. Charlotte could almost hear her eyes roll.

"I thought you wanted to go to that soccer tournament with Shelby tomorrow morning," he said in an innocent voice. "You'll never get up if you don't get to bed."

"I forgot about that," Hayley said, perking up.

"I guess you were having too good a time at the fish boil, huh?" Dylan said, smiling.

"The fish boil was lame," Hayley said. "There were only old people there."

"Gee, thanks, kid," Dylan said.

"Besides you," she said impatiently. "And Charlotte," she added.

"Thanks, Hayley. I'd hate to be in the lame category," Charlotte said, biting her lip.

"You're not lame. Your boat is way cool."

"Thanks." Charlotte twisted around to face the girl. "You're welcome to come see it again."

"Dad said you take people out to fish. Could I go with you sometime?"

"Sure, if it's all right with your dad."

"Cool."

They rode in silence for the rest of the short trip to Van Allen House. When they got there, Hayley climbed out. "Thanks for showing me your boat, Charlotte."

"You're welcome."

Dylan walked the girl to the door, opened it and stepped inside with her. He said something, then hugged her before watching her run up the stairs.

"She's a nice kid," Charlotte said when Dylan got into the car.

"Thanks. Like you said the other day, she takes after her mother."

"I apologize for that," Charlotte said, cringing. "That was nasty, and I didn't mean it. You'd just made me angry."

"I seem to be good at that." He glanced over at her as he stopped at the highway. "Are you always so volatile, or is it just me?"

The air in the car seemed to grow thin, and she struggled to breathe. "I'm normally a very even-tempered person," she said, unable to look away.

He pulled onto the highway with a jerk of the

wheel. "Then I guess I bring out the worst in you." He paused. "Or is it the best?"

"You bring out the irritation in me."

"Better than putting you to sleep."

Dylan would never put her to sleep. He infuriated her, annoyed her and provoked her.

He fascinated her.

And she knew better than to admit it to him.

"Let's just say you're one of a kind," she said.

"I get that a lot. I don't think it's a compliment."

"Wasn't meant to be." The car's tires hummed over the pavement and the waves rolled ashore from Green Bay. The lake was restless tonight, its white-caps illuminated by the moon.

As they drove through the town, heading toward the marina, she said, "You didn't have to take Hayley home first. You could have just dropped me off at the boat. Then you could have gone home together."

"Is that what you think I should have done?" he asked, a hint of laughter in his voice.

"It would have been more efficient."

"Efficiency is boring," he said. He reached out and skimmed her cheek, his fingers lingering. "Messy is so much more fun."

She wanted to press her hand over his, hold it against her skin. Instead she curled her hands together in her lap.

He ran his finger down her arm and drew a small circle on her wrist. When he took his hand away, she wanted to snatch it back.

"I had to drop Hayley off first. We never finished

what we started on your boat." His voice held a sensual promise, and she shivered.

"We didn't?" She tried to sound nonchalant. "You saw the whole boat, didn't you?"

His low laugh was full of promises. "I did. But there were places I want to examine more closely."

Charlotte swallowed, anticipation making her heart pound. She caught her breath. "What places?" she whispered.

"More private places," he murmured. "The kinds of places I couldn't explore if Hayley was with me."

CHAPTER SEVEN

CHARLOTTE'S TRUCK was parked far away from the one streetlight in the marina lot, its indistinct shape swallowed by the shadows.

"Welcoming place," Dylan said as he slammed the car door. It gave him the creeps—too quiet, too dark, too isolated. He didn't like the idea of Charlotte being here at night.

"I like the quiet," she said. "It's peaceful."

"It's spooky. Are you still sleeping on Gus's boat?"

"For another night or two. If nothing more happens, I'll go home."

"You mean you actually have a home somewhere?" he teased. "Other than your boat?"

"Believe it or not, I do."

"So I'm walking you to your boat tonight, instead of following you home?"

"You don't have to do that. I'll be fine." The weak light illuminated half her face. She looked mysterious and alluring. And nervous. The fire that had been smoldering inside him all evening roared to life.

"What about those other places you offered to

show me?" he asked, struggling to keep from touching her.

"You got the complete tour earlier," she said, but he saw the pulse leap in her throat.

"Not even close, Charlotte."

Her hand tightened on her keys. "All right. I guess you can stick around for awhile."

"I'd love to see it by moonlight."

He put his hand on her back, feeling her warm skin and the slight bumps of her spine, and steered her toward the dock. The scent of the water, fresh and wild, greeted them as they stepped onto the pier.

Her boat was dark and rocked gently on the waves. It didn't seem to bother Charlotte at all as she jumped onto the deck and unlocked the door. "Do you want a beer?"

"No, thanks. I have to drive back to Kendall's. But you go ahead."

He sat on the step to the cabin, and after a brief hesitation, she sat down next to him. As far away as she could get, he noted, amused.

"You made it sound as if Gus was on his deathbed," he said. "He looked tired, but otherwise pretty well."

She darted a quick glance at him, and he smiled to himself. Had she expected him to pounce on her?

"He's a lot better than he was a couple of weeks ago," she answered, relaxing against the wall.

"It must have been scary." He took her hand, smoothing his thumb over the calluses on her palm. It felt like Charlotte—tough on the surface, soft and vulnerable underneath. "It's always frightening when a parental figure is sick. Even when we're adults."

"It was," she said. She left her hand in his. "It was the first time Gus seemed mortal. The first time I thought about the possibility of him dying."

"He's not going to die."

"Not this time. But he has to slow down. He's not a young man."

"I doubt he'd appreciate you saying that."

She laughed. "No, he wouldn't. He's the most bullheaded man in Sturgeon Falls. But it's the truth."

"What about your parents? Do they live in Sturgeon Falls?"

"My mother lives in Green Bay," she said. "I have no idea where my father is."

"That's rough."

She shrugged. "I never knew him, so it's no loss."

"That makes it even more of a loss," he said.

She stared over the water. "How about you?"

"My mother passed away a year ago. Suddenly."

"I'm sorry. That must have been hard."

He didn't want to open that part of himself to her. "Yeah. I never knew my father, either."

"At least I had Gus. Did you have a father figure?"

Like her, he looked out at the black water, remembering. "My stepfather. He was a son of a bitch."

"You had a rough childhood."

"Better than some."

She tugged her hand away from his and stood. "This is a depressing way to end the evening."

He stood, as well. Waves splashed against the boat, rocking it gently. The moonlight shifted on her face with each roll of the boat, and the breeze carried a hint of her scent.

"Then we'll have to figure out a way to end on a more positive note," he said.

"Are you going to tell me a joke, Smith?" she asked, but she didn't sound as if she was going to laugh.

"That's not what I had in mind." They were almost touching. "And my name is Dylan. Say it, Charlotte," he whispered.

Her eyes, huge in the darkness, were unreadable. Her tongue slid along her lips, leaving a sheen of moisture behind. Need twisted inside him and his muscles tensed.

"Dylan." She stared at his mouth. "I thought you didn't kiss on a first date."

"Rules were made to be broken." He ran his finger along her mouth, then tucked his hands behind his back to keep from pulling her against him. "And besides, this is our second date."

"Don't break the rules for me," she said, her voice breathy.

"There's no one I'd rather break them for." He bent his head and brushed his lips over her mouth. He felt her tremble, and it stripped away what was left of his control.

Wrapping his arms around her, he pulled her close and kissed her again. She fit him perfectly, hip to hip, chest to chest. At first she stiffened, but then she sighed and wrapped her arms around his neck.

As the kiss became more passionate, he felt her moan, deep in her throat.

Holding her face in his hands, he nibbled at her lower lip until she opened her mouth. She tasted like passion and desire. His tongue tangled with hers and he pressed her against the side of the boat, needing to get closer.

She kissed him back, moving against him, pressing her breasts into his chest. Her arms tightened around his neck and she slid her hand through his hair, holding him.

He found her breast and caressed her through her blouse. She shuddered when he touched the hard tip with his thumb. He bent his head to brush his mouth over her other nipple. Even through the material, he felt her nipple tighten. Sucking lightly, he slipped his hand beneath her blouse. Her skin was soft and warm, and her muscles tensed beneath his fingers.

The texture of her skin intoxicated him. He wanted to touch her everywhere, to drink in her scent and her taste. He shoved her blouse up and kissed her abdomen, groaning as her muscles quivered beneath his lips. Needing to taste more of her, to see more of her, he reached for the buttons of her blouse, but she put her hand over his and stopped him.

"What's wrong?" he asked.

"Too much," she said, her chest rising and falling rapidly. "Too fast."

He struggled for control, finally releasing her. "Sorry," he said. "I shouldn't have let it go so far."

"There's nothing to apologize for. In case you didn't notice, I was right there with you," she said in a low voice. She smoothed her blouse into place, her trembling hands hovering over the damp spots. "I had to stop now. Before I couldn't stop."

"Charlotte." Her honesty destroyed his control. He reached for her, but she put some space between them. Strands of hair curled around her face, glowing in the moonlight. He could see faint marks from his five o'clock shadow on her cheeks. She would have the same marks on her belly.

She backed into the railing. "Sorry, Dylan," she said, still breathing heavily. "I wasn't expecting… I thought I could control…" She avoided looking at him. "Sorry."

"Don't be," he said. He brushed his lips over hers and felt her mouth soften. "You know how it feels to know I made you lose control? And you don't have to apologize for saying no."

"I don't jump into bed," she said against his mouth.

"Yeah, I got that." He trailed a finger down her cheek. "I'm devastated."

Her shoulders relaxed. "Even though you don't kiss on the first date?"

"I got carried away." He shoved his hands in his pockets. She wasn't the only one who'd almost lost control. He'd think about that later. "If I promise to keep my hands to myself, can we go out again?"

She shook her head. "I'm not sure that's smart."

"You can put me in handcuffs," he said. His blood heated again. "In fact, I'll insist on it."

"It's not *your* hands I'm worried about," she muttered.

He crowded her, intrigued by her honesty, fascinated by the desire in her eyes and her struggle to suppress it. "Then I don't see what the problem is."

She slipped past him to stand at the railing of the boat and look toward the lights of the city. "I'm attracted to you, Dylan. I don't want to be. I'm not looking for a relationship. And if I were, it wouldn't be with you. You don't even live here."

"Don't make this more complicated than it is," he said, wrapping his arms around her waist and pulling her against him. He nuzzled her hair, inhaling her sweet, tangy scent. "I'm glad you're not looking for a relationship, because I'm not, either. I was married once and I won't make that mistake again. Can't we just see where this goes?"

"I know where it's going, and I don't want to go there," she said. But she didn't move away.

He *did* want to go there. Very badly. "How about if I promise I won't touch you? Any moves that are made, you'll have to make them."

Her low chuckle drifted on the darkness. "I'm almost tempted to say yes, just to see how long that would last."

"You want to torment me? I'm up for that."

"I can tell," she said drily. "Go away, Dylan. I'm too tired to keep up with you tonight."

He kissed her again. "Good night, Charlotte," he

murmured against her lips. "Sleep tight." He smiled. "You're going to need your rest the next time I see you."

He jumped off the boat and walked down the pier, feeling her watching him the whole way to the car.

THE NEXT AFTERNOON Charlotte sat in the grass at the edge of the field at Sunset Park and watched Regan running down the length of it. The girl wore soccer shorts that hung below her knees and her shirt was so big it was slipping off her shoulder. But she had a fierce concentration on her face as she darted after the ball.

"All right, Regan," Charlotte yelled as the girl kicked it toward the goal. "Way to go!"

Regan almost smiled. Then she ran after the ball again.

"Hey, Charlotte." Kat sat beside her. "What are you doing here?"

"I came to watch my new niece play soccer," she said, watching Regan. "What do you think?"

"I think you're full of it," Kat said. "What's up?"

"Nothing," she protested. "When did you get so suspicious?"

"When you came to a six-year-old's soccer game on a Saturday during the summer," Kat retorted. "Spill."

Charlotte stared at the children on the field, not really seeing them. Instead, she saw Dylan, his eyes closed, kissing her.

It was a memory that had haunted her all day. And all night, as well.

"I had time between charters," she said, wrapping her arms around her knees. "I remembered Regan had a game."

Charlotte could feel Kat watching her as she stared at the kids. Finally she said quietly, "Tell me, CeeCee."

Charlotte's eyes burned at Kat's use of her childhood nickname. Blinking hard, she cleared her throat and said, "It's Dylan Smith. That reporter."

"What about him?"

"He's annoying me."

"Want me to beat him up for you?"

Charlotte choked back a laugh. "No, I can do that myself. What I can't do is get him out of my mind."

"And this is a problem why?"

Charlotte shot her friend an impatient look. "He's from Green Bay, Kat. He's here for a story, then he's going back to Green Bay. And on top of that, he wants to talk to…" She stopped, unsure if she wanted to tell Kat what Dylan really wanted.

"To whom?"

"To Gus," she said. "He wants to talk to Gus."

"So? What's wrong with that?"

"He wants to ask him about the Van Allen cherry orchard. He never worked there, did he?"

"I don't think so." Kat leaned back on her elbows. "I don't remember him ever talking about it. But he and Mom don't talk about the time before I was born." She grinned. "They say their lives began when I came along."

Charlotte laughed. This was why she'd come to Regan's game, she realized. To see Kat. "The curse of being an only child," she said lightly. "You think the world revolves around you."

"Doesn't it?" Kat laughed at Charlotte's expression and sat up. "Why don't you just tell Dad the guy wants to talk to him? It's not like he's on his deathbed."

"I probably would have, but now I'm worried about your mom." She picked a piece of grass and tore it in two lengthwise. "When I mentioned the orchard the other day, she acted odd. She even got upset that Dylan wanted to talk to Gus about it. Really upset. It was weird. I've never seen her act that way before."

Kat scooted closer to Charlotte. "I'm more interested in why you can't get him out of your mind."

Charlotte tossed the piece of grass to the ground. "I'm attracted to him," she admitted. "More than I want to be. More than I'm comfortable with."

"Well, hallelujah. It's about time. I was beginning to think that jerk Franklin had ruined you for other men."

"I don't want a relationship, Kat," she said in a low voice. "I want to concentrate on my business."

"I know Kyle did a number on you. But it's been three years. It's time to move on."

"I think I've moved on just fine. I took his boat and I'm making a business out of it. I'm getting repeat customers. I've made a life for myself."

"An empty life, if you ask me."

"Like you've got such a hot and heavy love life," Charlotte retorted.

"At least I have the excuse of a child to take care of." Kat waved at Regan. "What's your excuse?"

"I felt inadequate after the divorce." Charlotte hunched forward, resting her elbows on her knees, staring at Regan to keep the sudden tears from spilling. "How could I not?"

"Don't let that jerk define you," Kat said fiercely, wrapping her arm around Charlotte's shoulder. "Don't give him that power."

"He doesn't define me. But he made me cautious," Charlotte said. "I'm not about to jump into bed with another guy with my eyes closed."

"I hope not." Kat's smile was saucy. "It's so much more fun if your eyes are open."

Charlotte laughed. "Kat Macauley, I'm shocked. Do you kiss your mother with that mouth?"

Just then, Regan's team scored a goal. Charlotte and Kat jumped to their feet, cheering, and Kat let the subject drop. Thank goodness.

They were lounging in the grass again, talking quietly, when someone sat down beside Charlotte.

"Hey, ladies. Looks like you have an exciting game going here."

"Dylan." Charlotte bolted upright. "What are you doing here?"

CHAPTER EIGHT

"I HEARD THIS PARK is where the action is on Saturdays." Dylan's gaze lingered on her lips. Charlotte shivered at the flash of heat, then he leaned around her. "Hello, Kat. Regan looks like a real little soccer player."

"Apparently so." Kat smiled proudly. "I thought she needed more physical activity, so we signed up. She loves it."

"I've spent a lot of afternoons at soccer games," he said easily. "She's good for her age."

"Dylan, why are you here?" Charlotte asked.

He shrugged. "Nothing better to do, I guess. Hayley went with Kendall and Gabe and the girls to Shelby's tournament in Green Bay. So I'm on my own."

"And you chose to watch other kids play?"

"I didn't come for the soccer." He smoothed a finger over her hand. "I came to see you."

Trying to hide a smile, Kat stood up. "It's my turn for the after-game treats," she said, holding up a plastic container of quartered oranges. "I'm going to take them over to the girls."

Charlotte watched as her friend strolled away.

"What are you doing here? I told you I wasn't interested."

"You told me you didn't want to be interested."

"Same thing."

"You think so?" He smiled lazily. "Let's test that theory."

He edged toward her, staring at her lips, and she jumped to her feet. "For God's sake, Dylan. Behave yourself. We're in public. There are children here."

"Hmm, you may be right. Some things are best kept private, aren't they?" He got to his feet and crowded closer. "Can we go somewhere private, Charlotte?"

His voice was a dark whisper of sin in her ear, and she felt herself swaying. Then she jerked away. "Stop it, Dylan." Her voice was breathless, and she cleared her throat. "How did you find me, anyway?"

"You told Kat you might stop by Regan's soccer game, so I asked Kendall where it would be."

"I thought you had a story to work on."

"I need to talk to Gus before I can go any further. So I have time on my hands right now."

She glanced down at his hands, remembering how they'd felt last night. How he'd touched her. She snapped her head up. "Fine," she blurted. "I'll get you and Gus together. If you promise not to tire him out or upset him."

"Wow," he murmured, drawing her toward a stand of trees. "You're willing to let me talk to Gus in order to get rid of me?" He shook his head. "You must be desperate."

She was. If he didn't leave soon, if he kept coming around, she was afraid she was going to make a big mistake. "On Monday," she said, trying to sound offhand. "Gus needs a diversion, anyway. He's getting antsy."

"Monday sounds perfect." He took out his notebook and scribbled something. "So I can play for rest of the weekend."

"I can't." She glanced at her watch. "I have a charter at two. I can't stay much longer."

"It looks like the game is over." Dylan nodded toward the field where the kids were shaking hands.

"Good. I'll say hello to Regan and get going."

They walked back toward the sideline and watched Kat and Regan cross the field. Regan was holding Kat's hand and sucking on a piece of orange.

"Nice game, Regan," Charlotte said, smoothing the girl's hair. "Did you have fun?"

Without taking the orange out of her mouth, Regan nodded. Dylan crouched so their eyes were even. "Do you remember Hayley from last night?" he asked.

She nodded cautiously. The piece of fruit in her mouth looked like a giant orange smile.

"Hayley plays soccer, too," he said. "She loves soccer."

"Yeah?" Regan spit out the orange. "Me, too."

"I could tell. You kicked that ball real hard."

"I don't play very well," Regan said.

"It takes a lot of practice."

Charlotte was impressed that he hadn't lied to the girl. Most people would have told Regan that she was good, whether it was true or not.

Apparently Regan recognized his sincerity, as well. She nodded vigorously. "We practice a lot."

"Twice a week," Kat said.

Regan watched him seriously. "I like Hayley."

"Maybe Hayley can come to one of your games sometime." He glanced at Kat. "If it's okay with your mom."

Regan's face tightened. "Kat's not my mom." She kicked the soccer ball at her feet and sent it shooting into the trees.

Kat scooped Regan up and held her tightly, murmuring into her ear. Then she set her on the ground. "Let's go get that ball, honey. Charlotte has to leave." She shot Charlotte a distracted look.

Ill with shame, Charlotte watched them walk toward the trees. Kat bent to talk to Regan, and the girl nodded. Whatever Kat said seemed to help, because Regan let go of her hand and ran into the trees for her ball.

"I'm sorry," Dylan said. "I had no idea Regan wasn't her daughter."

"How could you know?" Charlotte should have told Dylan the night before at the fish boil. But she'd been so intent on keeping a barrier between them, so determined not to let him into her life in even that small way, she'd hurt Regan. And the last thing she wanted to do was cause any more pain to a child who'd already suffered more than her share.

"I need to apologize to them," he said.

He started for the trees and Charlotte grabbed his arm. "Don't," she said. With one more glance at her friend, she headed toward the parking lot. "Kat will take care of it."

"I upset Regan. I'm not going to just walk away."

"It's better if Kat talks to her," Charlotte said. She tugged on his hand and pulled him toward the cars. "Come on, Dylan. Let it go."

Most people would have been more than happy to walk away and forget the awkward moment. Dylan was determined not to. Feeling a flutter in her chest, Charlotte tightened her grip on his hand before letting him go. "I should have told you last night," she said. "You're making me ashamed I didn't."

"It wasn't any of my business."

"Maybe not. But last night you called Kat her mother, and I didn't say a word. I should have." She hesitated, but her conscience demanded that she level with him. "I wanted to keep you away from Gus and his family."

"I figured that out," Dylan said drily.

"Regan's mother died a few months ago. When she found out she was dying, she asked Kat to adopt Regan. The poor kid has had a rough time."

"Another fatherless kid." Dylan watched the pair emerge from the trees.

Charlotte had hated Regan's lost look when the child first lived with Kat. It reminded her of how she'd felt as a child, before she'd found the Macauleys. "Yes. Regan's mother gave Kat the father's name and Kat wrote to him, but she hasn't heard a thing. So the adoption should be final in a few months."

"Lucky kid."

Charlotte finally smiled. "I think Kat would say she was the lucky one."

They'd reached her truck, but she hesitated before opening the door. "Why did you really come here, Dylan?"

"Because I wanted to see you."

"And now you have," she said lightly. Her heart raced and her palms were damp. She yanked the door open.

He put his hand on her arm, and she paused. "What?"

"Have dinner with me tonight."

"I can't." She felt equal parts relief and regret.

"I know, you have a charter. Afterward."

"I'll be out late and I'll be too tired when I get back. I have to take the charter out alone."

"What about that kid you had with you the other day?"

"Steve? He's going to a wedding. I planned on taking the night off, but a group called this morning. I explained they wouldn't catch as many fish, but they didn't care. So we're going out." She'd needed the money.

"Isn't there someone else you can take with you?"

"Not at such short notice. Believe me, I tried."

"I could be your first mate. Why don't you let me help you out?" he said.

"Thanks for the offer," she said, almost desperate enough to consider it. "But Steve pilots the boat, and that isn't like driving a car. It would take too long to teach you how to do it."

"You wouldn't have to. I know how to handle a boat."

"You do?" She stared at him.

"My stepfather had a boat. I spent a lot of time on it." Something that might have been pain darkened his expression, but disappeared before she could identify it.

"I can't take advantage of you like that." But she was tempted.

"Charlotte, you can take advantage of me any way you like." His gaze grew intense and her skin felt scorched.

"I'm sure you have a million other things you could be doing this afternoon," she said, pulling away. "But thanks."

"Are you afraid of me?" he asked. His sultry voice belonged in the darkness, in a bedroom lit with candles. Not in a busy parking lot on a sunny afternoon.

"Of course I'm not afraid of you," she said. "I'm trying to give you a graceful out."

"Maybe I don't want an out, graceful or otherwise."

He stood too close, watching her perceptively. She *was* afraid. She didn't like knowing that a man could threaten her self-control. "Fine. Okay, I can use the help. Thank you." She slid into the truck. "Meet me at my boat at one-thirty."

She drove away and didn't let herself look back.

WHEN DYLAN REACHED Charlotte's boat a couple of hours later, she was checking her gear while eating a sandwich. She looked up from the outrigger she was adjusting and smiled.

"Come aboard. There are sandwiches in the refrigerator. Help yourself."

He grabbed one and then slid into the chair in front of the steering wheel. He forced down a sudden ripple of anxiety. He was an adult and this was a different boat. It was nothing like his stepfather's.

He sat there until he was comfortable with the controls, then headed to the deck to watch Charlotte. She clearly had a mental checklist she was following, and she moved efficiently from one task to the next.

"Thanks again for helping me," she finally said. "Any problems with the controls?"

She was brisk and businesslike, and he forced himself to be the same. "Nope. I should be able to take us wherever you want to go."

"Great. I'll take the helm until we're out of the harbor and heading toward the reef. While I'm doing that, your job is to make nice with the customers." She gave him a half smile, and it felt like she'd punched his chest. "I know you can handle that, Mr. Smooth. As soon as we're far enough out to drop the lines, we'll switch. I'll tell you where to go. Your job is to keep the boat moving steadily in that direction."

"Got it."

"Can you get a bag of ice for the cooler?" she asked, giving him directions to the machine.

"Sure."

By the time he returned with a bag of ice balanced on his shoulder, two couples were standing on the boat talking to Charlotte.

"This is Dylan Smith, the first mate," she said as he stepped onto the deck.

The men nodded their greetings. One of the women let her eyes drift over Dylan. "Hi, there. This boring fishing trip just became a lot more interesting."

She wore a tight white tank top and her skin was deeply tanned. The ball cap she wore pulled low over her blond hair didn't hide the avaricious gleam in her eyes. He nodded to her, opened the cooler and dumped in the ice.

"What next, Captain?" Dylan asked.

Charlotte's mouth quivered in a tiny smile. "You can untie us," she said, her voice a low murmur that sounded almost intimate. She glanced at the woman with the ball cap. "Thanks."

As they drifted away from the pier, she started the ignition and headed into the harbor. He took over once they cleared the breakwater.

He kept the boat on track, holding the speed steady as he followed Charlotte's directions. Once he relaxed, it was easier than he'd expected.

Charlotte was in constant motion. When he glanced back, he caught flashes of her legs, slender and muscular in baggy shorts. The wind made her T-shirt flutter and teased tendrils of hair out of her ponytail. As she stretched to set one of the fishing poles on an outrigger, explaining to the couples that they were allowed to have eighteen lines out, three for each person on the boat, her shirt pulled taut against her chest. The two men stared at her.

Charlotte must've seen him react because he only got halfway out of his seat before she'd come into the cabin under the pretense of looking at the sonar. "It's okay," she said quietly. "I'm used to it. It doesn't bother me."

"It bothers *me.*"

She squeezed his shoulder. "Don't worry about them." She glanced behind him and grinned. "Worry about yourself."

The blonde was stepping into the cabin. "My, uh, friend is feeling sick," she said.

Charlotte hurried out, and the woman sidled up to Dylan. "Hi," she said. "Dylan, right?"

"That's right," he said. One of the men was bent over the side of the boat, and Charlotte was standing next to him, holding his hat. When he stood up, she handed him a small towel and led him to the seat on top of the cooler.

Charlotte hurried through the cabin and down to the galley, where she grabbed a bottle of water. On the way back, she bumped him with her hip. "Slow down. It's starting to get choppy." She stepped out the door, handed the seasick man the water and crouched next to him, talking calmly.

Dylan eased off the throttle, trying to ignore the woman next to him. "What are you doing after we're finished here?" she asked.

"I'm going out to dinner. With Charlotte. If you want some nightlife suggestions, you'll have to talk to her. She's the expert."

"What are you an expert at?"

"I'm an expert on Charlotte."

The woman's expression hardened and she stalked away. A few moments later, one of the fishing poles twitched and Charlotte grabbed it. "Who's first?" she asked with a smile.

When no one immediately stepped forward, she thrust the pole at the blonde. "Here you go. Ladies first."

The line clicked as the fish ran with the lure, and Dylan could hear Charlotte telling the woman how to reel him in. Ten minutes later, Charlotte bent over the back of the boat with a net and scooped the fish out of the water. It flopped on the deck, gleaming silver in the sunlight.

"A king salmon," Charlotte said, using the fish club to dispatch it. "A nice one, too. This guy must be close to fifteen pounds." She turned to the blonde who'd reeled it in. "Want to take a picture, Cindy?"

The woman looked horrified, but she glanced at the men and finally said, "Sure."

Charlotte showed her where to hold the fish, then took a picture and tossed the fish into the cooler.

A few minutes later they got another hit, and then another after that. After they'd caught six fish, the seasick man stood up. "We need to go back," he said.

Charlotte looked at the four of them. "Is that all right with all of you? I don't give refunds if you cut the charter short."

"Yeah." The other man exchanged a look with his friend. "Take us back."

The sun dipped toward the horizon as they pulled into the harbor. Charlotte took the wheel again and brought them smoothly into the pier. As Dylan tied the boat, he watched her talking to the customers, making sure the seasick man was all right and explaining what they were going to do with the fish. The two women looked bored and the two men uncomfortable.

He'd had no idea she worked so hard on a charter.

She helped the women onto the pier. "Give me a hand with the cooler, Dylan. We'll get these fish filleted."

They carried the cooler to a bench near the marina, and Charlotte filleted them, one after another. Her knife flashed in the setting sun, and in fifteen minutes, all the fish were filleted and bagged.

After the customers had paid and were out of sight, Charlotte sank onto a chair. "Thank you," she said wearily. "I owe you an apology."

"What for?"

"I was snotty to you. I didn't want your help, but I knew I didn't have a choice. And you were great." She grinned. "Especially with the blond barracuda."

"Does that happen a lot?"

"You'd be surprised," she said. "Thank goodness Steve is mature enough to handle it."

"What about you?"

"I'm mature enough to handle it, too."

He looked toward the foursome who were getting into a sedan in the parking lot. "There was something off about that group."

She shrugged. "Getting seasick can ruin a day on the lake pretty quickly."

"It was more than that." He watched the car as it drove away. "They reminded me of those guys I chased off last week. The ones who gave you the creeps."

"They weren't the same guys."

"Maybe they came from the same place."

Charlotte stood up. "Maybe, but they're gone now, and they didn't have a chance to try and persuade me to see their point of view. You can go ahead," she said. "I'm going to finish cleaning up."

He followed her down to the boat, where she was spraying down the deck. After she hung the hose over the side, she said, "Haven't you seen enough of this boat for one day?"

"I've seen enough boats to last a lifetime. But I didn't come here to see the boat."

She dropped onto the step. "What do you mean?" she asked. "What do you have against boats?"

He looked out over the water. The sunset painted the sky orange and pink. "Nothing. I was just being a smart-ass."

She shifted so she could see him more clearly. "I don't think so. What?"

He didn't want to tell her. He didn't want to spill those ugly stories from his childhood. He didn't want to be that vulnerable.

But he'd seen her protecting Gus, helping Steve, taking care of the man who was sick on her boat. There was far more to Charlotte than her sometimes bristly exterior. He trusted her, he realized.

"Sit down," she said, her voice softer than he'd ever heard it. "Tell me."

CHAPTER NINE

HE HESITATED, his instincts telling him to run. He enjoyed chasing Charlotte, teasing her, trying to get her to open up to him.

Trying to get her to lead him to Gus.

But that didn't mean he wanted to spill his guts to her. Or for her to know his secrets.

He found himself sitting next to her on the step in the growing darkness. "My stepfather had a boat," he said, staring into the distance. "He insisted on taking me with him when he went out with it. Said he was going to teach me how to be a sailor." He shifted on the step. "Mostly what he taught me was how to yell and curse." And that mistakes would be rewarded with a slap on the side of the head.

He propped his elbows on his knees. "I had no interest in being a sailor. I hated those trips, hated everything about them." He shot her a look. "Mostly I hated my stepfather. And because he loved that boat, I wanted no part of it."

"So why did you come with me tonight?" she asked.

He shrugged. "You needed help. I know how to pilot a boat. Seemed like the logical thing to do."

"It was a generous thing to do." She skimmed her hand over his arm. "Especially since it dredged up old memories."

"I'm an adult. I can deal with it." He took her hand, rubbed his thumb against her palm. "Although it wasn't the quality time with you I was looking for."

"The only quality time on a charter is between me and the customers," she said.

"You really love this, don't you?"

She rested her arm on the side of the boat as it swayed in the water. "If I didn't, I'd have to be nuts to be doing it."

"How did you get started?"

His question hung in the air, and she tilted her head. "That was very slick, Dylan. How you made this conversation about me."

"I'm a boring guy," he said. "You're much more fascinating." He was getting sloppy if she saw through him so easily. "I assume Gus got you going with the boats?"

She hesitated, and he wasn't sure if she was going to allow him to change course. "Yes," she finally said. "Kat and I used to hang around the marina when we didn't have anything else to do. Kat never liked to fish—she got seasick as soon as the first wave hit. But I loved it."

"And you loved Gus."

"Yeah, I loved Gus. My mother wasn't home

much, so I spent most of my time with Kat and her parents. I used to pretend Gus and Frances were *my* parents." She glanced at him out of the corner of her eye. "I was jealous of Kat."

"Of course you were," he said. "You're human. It's normal to be jealous of people who have what we want."

"I wanted Gus and Frances." Her sadness made him want to reach for her.

"Kat always knew she wanted to be a doctor. The summer we were fifteen, she volunteered at the hospital. I hated the thought of being cooped up inside all day, so I hung around Gus's boat instead. He started taking me out on charters, and one day his first mate didn't show up." She smiled. "He let me replace the guy. The next summer, I got the job permanently."

"And now you have your own boat."

"I do." She stopped smiling. "You're not interested in hearing this ancient history. Hayley's waiting for you."

The ancient history was exactly what he needed to hear. But he'd probed enough for one night. "They're due back from the tournament in about an hour," he said. "Can you get a quick dinner?"

"Thanks, Dylan, but I need to get home. I have an early charter tomorrow morning."

She had dark circles beneath her eyes. "Call me if Steve doesn't show up."

"Steve will show up. He's been begging me for this job for two years," she said. She put her fishing rods inside the cabin, then locked the door. He jumped onto the pier and held out his hand to her.

She curled her fingers around his without hesitation and stepped out. He pressed his palm to hers and twined their fingers together.

"Good night, Dylan," she said, opening the door of her truck. "Come back on Monday around one. I'll make sure Gus is here."

"Thanks, Charlotte. I'll be here."

Her cell phone rang and she flipped it open. As she listened, she began to scowl. "That was damn stupid," she finally said. "What do you need me to do?"

She listened for a few more moments, then sighed. "You should be calling your parents. I know. I know. All right. I'll be right there."

"What happened?" he asked as she closed the phone.

"That was Steve," she said, grimacing. "He got into a fight at the wedding reception, and he needs me to bail him out of jail."

"Let me drive you," he said without thinking.

"Thanks, but this could take a while. I'll have to sweet-talk the sheriff into letting him go."

"You're tired. And I'm good at sweet-talking," he said.

"Tell me something I don't know. But you've already done me one huge favor today. I'm not about to ask you for another one."

"Please," he said quietly.

She jiggled her keys in her hand and finally sighed. "What about Hayley?"

"I'll call Kendall and tell her what's going on. I'm sure she'll take care of Hayley for me tonight. She's probably so tired she'll fall asleep on the way home."

"All right," she said after a long pause. "I guess I'd like the company."

Twenty minutes later, they pulled up to the sheriff's office. Dylan hadn't said much during the ride. "It's not too late to back out," she said, hoping he wouldn't. "You can just drop me off here."

"Not going to happen." He turned off the ignition. "I'd pay good money to watch you sweet-talk this guy."

She stared at the stone-and-glass building and braced herself to face Stan Godfrey. Dreading it. She was too tired to make nice. If the sheriff insisted on calling Steve's parents, she'd have a hard time keeping her temper. "Let's go."

A young woman sat at a desk behind glass inside the front door. "Hi. Can I help you?" she asked, smiling at Dylan.

"I'm here to see Sheriff Godfrey about Steve Jacobs," Charlotte said, more forcefully than necessary.

"Sure." The woman picked up the phone. "There's someone here about Jacobs."

She looked at Dylan again. "He'll be right out."

Charlotte sank onto one of the red chairs lined up against the wall. She heard footsteps approaching and struggled to find a smile.

"Charlotte!" The man stepping into the room looked surprised. "What are you doing here?"

"Brady," she said, relieved. Thank goodness it was her old high school friend instead of Godfrey. She jumped up and kissed him on the cheek. "I'm glad you're here. I came to bail out Steve Jacobs."

Brady sighed. "He was supposed to call his parents. The sheriff made that clear to all of us the last time he was arrested."

She took Brady's arm and led him to a corner of the room where neither the receptionist nor Dylan could overhear them. "You know as well as I do why he didn't call his parents," she said in a low voice. "I'm not going to let that happen. Are you?"

The deputy's mouth thinned. "No, I won't. I'll release him to you. But you need to pay in cash," he said equally quietly. "And make sure no one can read your signature."

"I should have enough money. My customers paid cash today." She showed him a stack of bills. "Where's the sheriff?"

"He's gone for the night," Brady said. "Come on back."

Charlotte glanced at Dylan, who frowned. She could see he had questions. "We'll be out in a minute, all right?"

The deputy followed her gaze. "This guy is with you?"

"It's all right," she said, pushing him toward the offices. "Don't worry about him."

They turned a corner and she saw Steve slumped in a chair next to a desk. There was a dark red splotch on the sleeve of his shirt, he had a bruise on the left side of his face and his eyes were bloodshot. He looked away, but not before she'd seen his shame.

Brady grabbed her by the arm as she walked toward Steve. "Save the lecture for later," he said.

Keeping one eye on Steve, she quickly filled out the forms Brady shoved at her, signed her name in an illegible scrawl, then counted out three hundred dollars. "All right? Is that it?"

"Get out of here," Brady muttered, sticking the money in a box in the desk. "And you." He pointed at Steve. "I don't know what the hell you were thinking, but it better not happen again. If it does, your ass is grass. And so is Charlotte's. The sheriff won't like it if he finds out she paid your bail." His expression hardened. "You understand?"

"Yes, sir," Steve said, licking his lips. Charlotte saw a smear of dried blood in the corner of his mouth. "Trust me, it won't happen again."

"I hope not." Brady jerked his head at the door. "Go."

Steve staggered when he stood up and Charlotte reached out and steadied him. Holding him firmly, she steered him around the corner. Dylan opened the outer door when he saw them, and in seconds the three of them were in the parking lot. She shoved Steve into the backseat of Dylan's car and scrambled into the front.

Dylan climbed into the car without saying a thing. He started it up and drove out of the parking lot, a little too fast.

"Go back to the marina," she told Dylan. Wincing at the harshness of her tone, she added, "Please."

The marina parking lot was deserted. Dylan stopped the car and started to get out, but she stopped him. "Wait. I came here only because I knew there wouldn't be anyone around. We needed someplace to talk."

Swiveling in her seat, she stared at Steve, who wouldn't raise his head. Finally she said as gently as she could, "What happened?"

"Junie was there," he said. His voice trembled. "With Chip Schlutter. Chip was ragging on me all night. One dig after another. When he started in about how Junie gave the best…" He swallowed and even in the semidarkness Charlotte could see his face redden. "He was talking about private stuff. And Junie was embarrassed. I could tell. So I punched him."

"Oh, Steve," she said softly. "Why didn't you just walk away?"

"I tried, Charlotte." He lifted his head. "I walked away more than once. But that asshole kept following me. He wouldn't stop." He swallowed. "He made Junie cry. The next thing I knew, I'd punched Schlutter and he was on the ground."

"And you'd been drinking."

He sighed. "Yeah, I'd been drinking."

"You'd better sleep on the boat tonight," she said and Dylan took her hand. "You can't go home like this."

"I know." The boy's voice was so quiet she could barely hear him.

"When you're sober, we're going to talk again," she said. "And you know what we're going to talk about."

Steve rubbed his face. "Yeah, I know."

"You were damn lucky Brady Morgan picked you up instead of Sheriff Godfrey."

"I'm sorry I had to call you. Really sorry. And you were on a date. I'm sorry, man," he said to Dylan.

"Don't worry about me. I took your place on Charlotte's boat tonight," Dylan said casually. "And I'd like to do it again. So it's no skin off my nose if you screw up."

Steve's head snapped up. "Are you firing me?" he asked Charlotte, panicked.

She squeezed Dylan's hand. Somehow he'd known exactly the right words to say. "Not yet," she said. "But if you don't get some help, I'll have to. What would I have done tomorrow morning if you were in jail?"

"I haven't missed a day of work," he said, his voice rising.

"Not so far. But if you keep getting drunk and beating people up, sooner or later you're going to."

Steve flopped back against the seat. "I'll do whatever you tell me to do, Charlotte."

She let Dylan go and stepped out of the car, helping Steve out. "I've heard that before."

"I mean it this time," he said, stumbling. "I do."

"We'll see." Dylan took Steve's other arm as they headed down the pier toward her boat. "I'll be here at five a.m. I expect you to be ready to go."

"I will be," he said, nodding like a bobble-head doll. "I promise."

Charlotte unlocked the door and watched Steve lurch down the stairs. He bumped into the wall, then abruptly opened the door to the head. When she heard water running, she shut the door and slid down to sit on the step.

Dylan sat and wrapped his arm around her. She slumped against him. "Thank you," she said. "For coming with me. For knowing what to say to Steve."

"You seemed to know how to handle him just fine by yourself," he answered.

"Knowing what to say is one thing. Getting him to do it is something else entirely." She shifted beneath his arm but didn't move away. It was…nice, having someone to lean on. Even if it was only for a few minutes. "You hit exactly the right note, hinting you were after his job."

The arm he'd draped over her shoulder tightened, and his fingers brushed her skin. "Guys are competitive. You said he'd been begging you for a job for two years. Then when he gets arrested and has to call you to bail him out, he finds out I worked in his place. He's got to be terrified you're going to give me the job."

"I'd never do that. And Steve knows it."

"He's drunk," Dylan said, his voice flat. "He's not thinking straight. I figured out a long time ago that when you deal with drunks, you use whatever works. He may not remember a whole lot in the morning, but I bet he'll remember I want his job."

She allowed herself to remain in the circle of his arm. Just for a few more minutes, she promised herself. Then she'd leave. "How do you know so much about dealing with drunks?"

He didn't answer for a long time. Finally he eased away from her and stood up. "It's a life skill, Charlotte. Everyone knows at least one drinker. You must get your share of them on this job."

"A few. But they don't give me much trouble. Most of them end up with their heads hanging over the side of the boat. Alcohol and boats don't mix real well." He hadn't really answered her question, and now he was edging toward the pier. Apparently he liked to be the one asking the questions. "Thanks again, Dylan. I'll see you Monday."

He stopped. "You're not staying here tonight, are you?"

"No." She adjusted the rubber pad on top of the cooler. Anything to look busy. The boat swayed and she widened her stance. "I'm going to check the boat once more, then I'm going home and sleeping in my own bed for what's left of the night."

"I'll walk you to your truck."

"Not necessary," she said.

"I don't mind waiting until you're finished."

"Go home, Dylan. I'm fine."

He sat down on the rail. "What's wrong, Charlotte?"

"Nothing's wrong." She bent over the railing and examined the anchor rope. "I'm trying to be considerate. You spent most of your day helping me."

"It was my choice. No one twisted my arm." He paused. "Is that what's bothering you? That you had to ask for help?"

"I'm not afraid to ask for help when I need it." She straightened. "I thought we were getting to know each other."

"I thought so, too. So what's the problem?"

"It goes both ways, Dylan. You shut me down pretty darn fast when I asked how you knew about dealing with drunks. And you sure didn't want to give me any details about why you don't like boats. I felt like I was dragging every word out of you." And he still hadn't told her he was looking for his father.

"I told you I don't do relationships," he said defensively. "Why do you think Hayley's mother and I got divorced?"

"So you just go through life screwing women and moving on when they want to know more than your last name?"

"It's worked for me so far."

"It doesn't work for me."

"You're one to talk. You haven't exactly been an open book, yourself."

"So why do you bother?" she asked.

He smiled in the dark, and her heart constricted. "Maybe I'm as stubborn as you are, Charlotte," he finally said. "Maybe I think you're worth it. Or maybe I'm just an idiot." He stood up from the railing. "I thought you wanted to get home and get to sleep. Are you going to let me walk you to your car? Or are you going to keep stalling?"

She stepped onto the pier. She couldn't tell what he was thinking as they walked to her truck. Just as she couldn't tell what he'd been thinking earlier, when he'd told her that he didn't like boats.

She was thinking it was a damn shame that she and Dylan were so alike.

CHAPTER TEN

"THANK YOU FOR AGREEING to talk to me," Dylan said as he shook Gus's hand.

"Frances didn't want me to." Gus frowned, settling onto the couch in Charlotte's boat. "She said she didn't want me to get worked up. But it was a good excuse to come to the marina." He glanced at Charlotte, who was tying lures at the galley table. "Maybe Charlotte and I will take the boat out after."

"Not going to happen," Charlotte said without looking up.

Gus's gaze lingered on Charlotte, and Dylan swallowed around an unexpected lump in his throat. Charlotte was damn lucky she had Gus in her life. The love he saw in Gus's eyes, the close relationship the two shared, only fueled Dylan's determination to find out about his own father.

Gus settled back. "Are you the fellow Charlotte brought to the fish boil last Friday?"

"That was me," Dylan replied.

"You sniffing around my girl?"

"Gus!" Charlotte lifted her head and narrowed her eyes. "Watch it."

"Who else is gonna ask him his intentions?"

"I know what his intentions are," Charlotte said. A smile tugged at her mouth. "I can deal with them myself."

"I let you down last time. I'm not going to do it again."

Charlotte sighed. "Gus, what happened with—" She stopped and shook her head. "That was *not* your fault. Let it go."

Dylan sat and watched, willing them to keep talking. He wanted very badly to know what Gus was talking about. He suspected it would answer a lot of questions about Charlotte.

"I'm just watching out for you," Gus protested. "Seems like you'd be grateful."

Charlotte smiled, and Dylan's heart ached to see the love and understanding in her expression. "I am grateful. I adore you, Gus, but let it go. Okay?"

Gus shot a look at Dylan. "You never brought anyone to the fish boil before."

"He was looking for local color," Charlotte said, raising an eyebrow. "I figured it didn't get any more colorful than the gang at the VFW."

"Charlotte thinks I should apologize," Gus said, throwing Dylan a challenging look.

"No apology necessary," Dylan said easily. "I have a daughter, and you can bet I'm going to grill any guy she brings around."

"Hear that, missy?" Gus crowed. Dylan suppressed a laugh.

"Don't encourage him, Smith." Charlotte sighed.

"So what do you want to know about Sturgeon Falls?" Gus asked.

"First of all, tell me something about the attack on your boat. Who do you think is responsible?" He pulled the notebook out of his pocket.

He sensed Charlotte's abrupt attentiveness, and he smiled. He'd promised her he'd do a story about the vandalism and he always kept his promises.

"Punk kids," Gus said.

"Do you think it could have anything to do with the developers who want to buy the marina?"

Gus snorted. "Who knows? But if they were behind it, they're damn stupid. A stunt like that is only going to make me more determined not to sell."

"Have you thought about getting guards for the boats?"

"Guards?" Gus shook his head. "You know how much that costs? Most of us are barely making it as it is."

Dylan looked up from his notebook. "Did Charlotte tell you about the four guys she took out the other day? Not real interested in fishing, but very interested in her. They tried to get her off the boat. I wondered if they might have something to do with the developers."

"What?" Gus shifted on the couch and glared at Charlotte. "She didn't tell me about that."

"They were tourists," she said. "That's all."

"How can you be sure of that?" Dylan asked.

"I can't be," she admitted. "But they haven't come back, so there's no point in worrying about them."

"They were pressuring her to go out with them?" Gus asked Dylan.

Before he could answer, Charlotte said, "Gus, I'm not going anywhere with a customer. You know that."

"Yeah, I know. Be careful anyway."

"I always am."

Dylan watched the silent communication that ensued between the two of them and felt like an intruder. He cleared his throat. "Gus, what I really wanted to ask you about is the cherry orchards. Specifically the Van Allen orchard. Bertie told me you'd worked there one summer."

Gus went still. "I worked there one season. A few months. What could I possibly tell you?"

"Do you mind if I take notes?" Dylan asked, holding up his notebook.

"Take all the damn notes you want. I don't know anything about the orchard."

"Why did you choose to work there?"

"I didn't. My father did."

"Really?" Dylan scribbled in his notebook and noticed that Charlotte was watching them. "Why was that?"

"I wanted to fish. That's all I ever wanted to do. But I couldn't swing the financing for a boat. My father agreed to co-sign a loan with me if I'd give something else a chance first. He knew Stuart, so he got me a job in the office."

"Why not just sign the loan?"

"He didn't think running a charter was the right

kind of job. He didn't understand it. Frances and I saved every penny we made, but the bank wouldn't give me the loan without a co-signer. So I caved in." Gus shifted uncomfortably.

"And?"

"And I hated it. Hated being inside during the summer. Hated the boring, repetitive work. I snuck outside every chance I got."

Dylan leaned forward in his chair. "What kinds of jobs did you do in the orchard?"

There was a beat of silence, then Gus shrugged. "Whatever needed doing. I wasn't picky." Gus shifted again and didn't meet his gaze.

"So you spent time with the workers?"

"What the hell kind of question is that? Of course I did. I said I was out in the orchard, didn't I?"

"Do you remember any of them?"

Gus stood up, shoved his hands into the pockets of his worn khaki pants and stared out the door. Dylan couldn't see his face. "It was a long time ago," he finally said. "There were a lot of people working there."

"Do you remember seeing Van Allen out in the orchard, or did he work mostly in the office?"

"Stuart? Yeah, he was out there. He didn't stay in the office much. Why do you want to know?" Gus asked.

Dylan was careful not to look over at Charlotte. She was getting too good at reading him. "I want to get a feel for the owners. How they ran their businesses."

"Stuart was a hands-on guy," Gus said. "He loved that orchard. He could do every single job there, better than most of the workers."

"So he had a lot of contact with the people who worked for him."

"Just said he did."

"Do you remember what year you worked there?" Dylan asked.

"It was thirty-one, thirty-two years ago. I'd have to sit down and figure it out," Gus said. Dylan saw his fists bunch in his pockets. "Is it important?"

"Probably not," Dylan said easily, watching Gus's stiff back. "If it turns out to be, I'll get back to you." He pretended to write something down. "Did you only work there one season?"

"That was all I could take. I stuck it out for that one summer, my father co-signed the loan for my boat and that was the last time I thought about the Van Allen orchard."

He wanted to ask about Stuart's relationships with the female migrant workers, but he suspected Gus wouldn't be forthcoming in front of Charlotte. "Thanks for your help, Mr. Macauley. Can I buy you a beer sometime?"

"Maybe. Depends on how you treat Charlotte."

Charlotte eased to her feet and headed up the stairs. "Take it easy, Gus. I get to decide for myself how I want to be treated."

"Never hurts to know someone is watching," he answered as he ambled out the door and down the stairs. "Remember that, Mr. Reporter."

Charlotte stepped around him to help Gus over the side of the boat. She stood watching until he disappeared from view.

"Well," she said brightly as she turned around. "That was awkward."

"Don't worry about it," he said. "It's kind of sweet."

"Really? You thought it was sweet to be told not to lay a finger on me?"

Dylan grinned. "He's too late for that, isn't he?"

Pink colored her cheeks. "You know what I mean."

"He doesn't want me to hurt you," Dylan said. "I'm glad you have someone who cares enough to warn me off."

"Gus never hesitates to say what he thinks."

"I wondered where you got it," he said. "Now I know."

"I hope I'm a little more smooth than that," she said. "Gus takes blunt to a whole new level."

"What did he mean when he said he let you down the last time?"

She crossed her arms over her chest and rested against the glass door of the cabin. "I'll tell you what, Dylan. You explain what you're really doing here in Sturgeon Falls. Why you're really asking questions about Stuart and the Van Allen orchard. And I'll tell you why Gus thinks he let me down."

His instinct was to make a joke and let it drop. The search for his father was too personal.

She'd been right earlier. He wanted to be the one asking the questions, not answering them.

But in spite of what he'd said about not wanting a relationship, he wanted to know more about Charlotte. About what made her tick. And he suspected that knowing what had happened to her, what Gus had failed to protect her from, would provide some of the answers.

"Okay," he said, noting her surprise. And the faint uneasiness that followed it. "We'll swap secrets."

Charlotte pushed away from the wall. "Let's get out of here," she said. "There's no privacy."

"Sounds good. Where do you want to go?"

She looked like she wanted to change her mind. She took a deep breath and said, "We can go to my place. We won't be interrupted there."

"Fine." He'd wondered where she lived, what her house would look like. He jumped onto the pier and held out his hand, and she took it.

Holding her hand casually, as if he'd just forgotten to let it go, he asked, "I've been wondering what happened with Steve on Sunday."

She let out a small breath, as if she'd been afraid he'd immediately start questioning her about what Gus had said. "He was awake when I got to the boat at five. Dressed and vertical. He'd already started the prelaunch chores. And he was fine during the trip." She smiled. "He turned green when the waves got rough toward the end of the trip, but he never said a word. And even though he was still green, he filleted the fish we caught."

"Have you had that talk with him?"

"No." She sighed. "He took off as soon as we'd

finished. Said he'd be back to talk later, but he never showed up."

"What are you going to do?" he asked, curious.

"I'm going to hunt him down," she said. "Then we'll have a heart-to-heart."

She was already working too many hours of the day, but she wanted to help her employee. "He's a lucky guy, to have you for a boss," Dylan said.

"I'm impressed," she said. "You didn't ask me any questions. Where is that reporter's curiosity?"

"Barely held in check," he admitted. "But Steve is none of my business. I wouldn't ask you to betray a confidence."

"Thank you." She sounded surprised, and he frowned. Was he that pushy?

"You want to follow me to my house?" she asked, letting go of his hand and opening the door of her truck.

"Sure."

Swinging onto the seat, she said, "See you in a few minutes."

It was more than a few minutes. Her house was south of town on County U. The houses stood far apart on large lots that were mostly covered with trees. She finally pulled into the driveway of a small, white Cape Cod-style house with black shutters.

She looked nervous as she got out of the truck, but she headed for the front door and unlocked it.

He walked into the living room and stopped abruptly. The house was a shock. There was color everywhere, from the jewel-like blue of the couch to the red and yellow pillows piled on it to the Oriental rug on the wood floor. The walls were a buttery yellow, and they were covered with paintings that seemed to shimmer with life in the afternoon sun.

"Wow," he said. "This is beautiful. And I love the paintings."

"Gus's wife, Frances, painted them," she said as she shut the door. "Can I get you something to drink?"

"A cola would be great."

She disappeared into the kitchen, returning quickly with two glasses. "Have a seat."

After they'd settled on the couch, she hesitated for a moment, then said, "You go first."

"I figured you'd say that." He turned the glass in his hand, the condensation cool against his fingers. It had been a long time since he'd confided in anyone.

"You were right," he said abruptly. Best to jump right in. "I'm not really doing a story on the orchards. But I *am* trying to find out as much as I can about Stuart Van Allen."

"How come?" she asked softly.

His hand tightened on the glass, then he set it on a coaster. "Because I think he's my father."

"Why do you think that?"

Her expression was sympathetic and encouraging. But not surprised. "You already knew."

"Kendall said you were looking for your father. And you weren't interested in anyone besides Stuart."

Feeling deflated and defensive, he asked, "So why bother asking if you already knew?"

"Why do you think, Dylan?"

She held his gaze steadily and he jiggled his leg, unsettled by her compassion. "Because you want to jump my bones but need to know my pedigree first?" he said, his smile strained.

Her understanding was almost more frightening than the sympathy. She shook her head.

"I don't need to know a guy's pedigree before I jump his bones. But I do need to know the guy."

"Well, there you have it. I'm a bastard who doesn't even know who his father was."

"That's an ugly word. We're a lot more than the sum of our parents," she said.

"Easy to say when you know who they are."

"Tell me about your mother." She scooted closer and reached for his hand. He took comfort in the feel of the calluses on her palms, the strength in her grip.

"She was a migrant worker at the orchard the summer I was conceived. She'd come from Appalachia, ran away from home when she was sixteen." He looked out the window. "For all the usual reasons. Farm work was all she knew."

"She never told you who your father was?"

"He was an important man at an orchard. That's all she would say. She wouldn't talk about it while she was married to my stepfather. Then right after their divorce she had a stroke and died. There was nothing in her papers to tell me who he was. All I found was a label from an old cherry crate. From the Van Allen orchard."

"I'm sorry, Dylan."

He shrugged. "That's my story. I know Stuart is dead, but I want to know for sure he's my father. For myself, but also for Hayley. She deserves to know where she came from."

"She came from you. Isn't that enough?"

"Our past makes us who we are," he said.

"We make ourselves into who we are. Even if Stuart is your biological father, he played no role in your life. All he contributed was a set of genes. Your mother and stepfather are the people who shaped you."

"I don't want the legacy of my stepfather," he said. "I want to erase him. I want to think things would be different if I'd grown up knowing that a decent man was my father."

"Decent?" He could read the pity in her expression. "Stuart was certainly an important man, like your mother said, but I'm not sure about decent. According to the stories I've heard, he chased anything in a skirt."

"My mother thought he was good." He touched the medal he wore beneath his shirt. "She kept the label from the cherry crate. And some other things he gave her."

"Maybe he was," she said softly. "Have you talked to Kendall about him?"

"Not yet. I wanted to wait until I was more certain he was the one."

"I hope she can give you what you need."

He did, too. "If she can't, this trip hasn't been a waste." He reached out and touched her face. "I met you."

"So I'm the booby prize?" she said with a tiny smile.

"No. Maybe you're the real prize," he said, surprised that he meant it.

She leaned into his hand, then eased away. "Let's see what you think after you hear my story."

CHAPTER ELEVEN

CHARLOTTE UNTANGLED her hand from Dylan's. She needed her mind to be clear. She didn't think clearly when Dylan was touching her.

Dylan gulped a mouthful of soda. "Okay," he said. "Tell me what Gus was talking about."

Charlotte picked up one of the pillows from the couch and hugged it. "He's talking about my ex-husband."

"Your ex-husband? You never said anything about being married."

"It's not one of my happier memories." She closed her eyes. She would *not* cry. "We were married for ten months."

"What happened?" His glass clinked as he set it down.

"I caught him having sex with another woman. I kicked him out and filed for divorce."

"Your husband cheated on you? He must have been a complete idiot. What was wrong with him?"

"According to him, the problem was with me." She looked away, remembering the humiliation and pain. And Kyle's casual dismissal of her shock, then his scorn and mockery.

"And why does Gus think he's responsible?"

"Because he introduced us."

"Oh. Yeah, I see why he'd think it was his fault."

"You're as bad as Gus," she said, getting up and standing in front of the window. "He introduced us. That was all. Anything that happened afterward was my decision. Including marrying the jerk."

His hands kneaded her shoulders, working away the tension. She wanted to lean into him, but she stood rigidly straight, unsure of herself. "How on earth could he have known Kyle would cheat on me?" she demanded. "He doesn't have a crystal ball."

"I'll bet Gus kicked his rear end around the block when he found out." He nuzzled her neck, making her catch her breath. "Does the guy live in Sturgeon Falls? Because I'd like a shot at him myself."

"No," she said, drawing an unsteady breath. "He was from Chicago. He thought it would be fun to be a charter captain. I got the boat in the divorce settlement, and he went back to Chicago."

"Too bad."

"I wouldn't let Gus beat him up, and I wouldn't let you, either."

"Why not?"

"I don't want you to get hurt. He's not worth it."

"See, that's where you don't understand guys." He looped his arms around her waist and pulled her against him. "It's a matter of pride that we kick the ass of anyone who hurts our women." He nipped at her ear, making her shiver.

"I'm not your woman, Dylan," she said, but she snuggled nearer.

"You don't think so?" He trailed his mouth over her hair, then tugged at the band that held it in a ponytail. It tumbled free down her back and he tangled his fingers in it. "Hmm. Let's test that theory."

She shivered again as he nibbled on her neck. He stroked her stomach lightly, then slipped beneath her blouse. She closed her eyes. The hard ridge of his erection burned into her, and she reached around to grasp his hips.

"We fit together perfectly," he whispered, his breath caressing her ear. "I dream about you at night, Charlotte. Do you want to know what we're doing in my dreams?"

Yes. Wildness swept over her. "Tell me."

His mouth brushed her ear. "I'm touching you. Tasting you. Kissing you. Every inch of your body. And you're doing the same to me."

She wanted to turn in his arms and make his fantasy come true. Make her own fantasies come true. But she hesitated, still awkward.

"What about you?" he whispered. "Do you dream about me, Charlotte?"

She remembered the vivid, erotic dreams that haunted her sleep, the aching need that lingered even after she woke up. "Yes," she said, her voice barely a whisper.

His arms tightened around her. "Tell me what you dream about."

She gazed, unseeing, at the wall, furious at her insecurity, struggling to overcome it. "I dream about us." She swallowed hard. "Making love."

His hands trembled on her stomach as he stroked her skin. "What else?"

"Isn't that enough?"

She felt the low rumble of his laugh against her cheek. "Details, Charlotte. I want details." He brushed his hands over her breasts. "How can I make your fantasies come true without them?"

"You're doing a pretty good job," she managed to say. He traced slow, lazy circles that shot fire through her, even through the flimsy material of her bra. She was desperate to feel his hands on her bare skin. Finally, when she was about to go mad, she reached behind and fumbled with the clasp.

"I thought you'd never ask," he murmured. He undid her bra, then cupped her breasts in his hands, brushing his thumbs over her nipples. She couldn't suppress a moan.

"It's not enough, Charlotte. I love the way you feel. Your skin is so soft. So smooth. But I need to taste you."

His hands left her breasts and he turned her around to him. Holding her face in his hands, he kissed her. Heat and desire, barely held in check, swept over her. His chest rose and fell against hers and his breathing was ragged. She melted into him, lost in the solid strength of him. In his need for her.

His kiss went on and on, until she could barely stand. Finally he tore his mouth from hers. "Charlotte," he gasped, his voice shaky. "You're making me crazy. I have to slow down."

She pulled his head down, desperate to feel his mouth on hers again, but after barely a taste, he eased away. When he began to undo the buttons on her shirt, her insecurity caused her to grab at his hands. He merely kissed her palms and continued. When the last button was undone, he smoothed her shirt open and cool air swept over her chest. Her bra dangled on her arms, exposing her breasts.

"Beautiful," he murmured, running his hands over them. "You're so beautiful."

He took one nipple in his mouth and suckled it gently. A cry burst from her mouth and she stumbled. Her legs couldn't hold her weight.

Dylan blew gently on the breast he'd been sucking, sending another shock through her. "I need you to tell me something, Charlotte."

"What?" she asked, breathless.

He led her to the couch and she sat, her legs trembling. He held her so she couldn't look away. "When you caught your husband cheating on you, he told you it was your fault. What did he mean?"

A chill washed over her. She pulled her blouse together. "He was trying to hurt me," she said. "That's all."

"I don't think so," he said softly. "Tell me."

She was humiliated all over again. "That's not exactly the kind of thing I want to share with you."

"Do you want me to guess?"

He could tell. Oh, God, she knew this had been a mistake. She fumbled for the buttons of her blouse, her hands shaking and her eyes burning.

He put his hands over hers. "Did he tell you that you were lousy in bed? That was why he had to have other women?"

She tried to push his hands away, but he entwined their fingers together. "When a man tells a woman that—" he kissed her "—it means he's a selfish jerk. He knows nothing about making a woman happy, and doesn't care. He's only interested in satisfying himself." He kissed her again. "You didn't believe him, did you?"

She'd had nothing to compare Kyle with. "Of course not."

He smiled against her mouth. "I didn't think so. You're too smart to buy that kind of lie." He bent and nuzzled her shirt aside. "But just in case you have a few lingering doubts, I'm going to prove he was wrong." He licked her breast and she shuddered. "Okay?"

She couldn't answer. But he didn't seem to need a response. Easing her blouse and bra from her arms, he dropped them to the floor. Then he eased back to look at her. Heat rose in her face and she wanted to cover herself with her hands.

He must have seen it in her eyes. "No," he whispered. "You're beautiful." His gaze swept her body. "Perfect."

He bent his head to her breast again. While he

kissed her and swirled his tongue around her, he unbuttoned her jeans and slid them down her legs. In moments, she was wearing only a skimpy swatch of lace.

"Did he make you come?" Dylan asked, moving to her other breast.

Shocked, she opened her eyes to find him watching her. His expression was intense with need. For her, she realized with a surge of desire.

"Did he?"

"Why are you talking so much?" she asked, reaching for him. "I don't want to talk anymore."

"I'll take that as a no," he said with another slow kiss. "He was a loser, Charlotte."

"Who was?" she gasped.

Grinning, he slipped down her body, kissing her as he went. When he reached her panties, he slowly pulled them down her legs.

Naked in front of Dylan, she felt wild and sexy and wicked. With the sun shining behind him, Dylan glowed golden in the light. As he tossed her panties away, he grinned up at her again and pressed his mouth between her legs.

She arched against him, and he held her steady, licking and tasting. When he suckled her gently, she exploded in a climax.

Overwhelmed, she reached for Dylan. He gathered her close and held her tightly, murmuring her name. Eventually her awareness returned, along with her self-consciousness. She was spread out on the couch like a buffet, and Dylan had devoured her like a starving man.

What was she supposed to do next? Tucked against him, she could feel his erection against her abdomen, even though he was fully dressed. Why hadn't he undressed? Was he waiting for her to do it?

She hated being unsure of herself.

"That was kind of one-sided," she whispered, sliding her hands over his back. "I don't want to be the selfish one."

"You don't think I enjoyed that?" He lifted his head. "Didn't I tell you that was my fantasy? To touch you and taste you everywhere?"

"That was only part of your fantasy," she said, studying his face. "I thought there was another part of it. Something about me doing the same thing to you. But you still have your clothes on."

"That's because I don't have any condoms with me," he said. "I'm guessing you don't have any, either."

He waited and she shook her head. "Nope. No condoms," she said, hating that she was so inexperienced, knowing he could tell.

"Then I have to leave my clothes on. If I take them off, we'll definitely need condoms."

"There are some things we don't need condoms for," she said.

"Yeah?" He grinned at her. "Like what?"

Her face flamed and she reached for his shirt to hide her awkwardness. Her fingers shook as she unbuttoned it, then she pressed her mouth against the warm skin and hard muscle of his chest.

His groan gave her confidence, and she swirled her tongue around his flat nipples, pushing aside the silver disc that hung on a chain around his neck. When he groaned again, she ran her teeth over him. He shoved his hands into her hair to hold her in place.

She was working her way down his chest to his flat belly when her cell phone rang. She froze.

When she didn't move, Dylan grabbed the phone and looked at the screen. "Charlotte, it's Steve," he said.

"I can call him back," she said, pressing her fingers into the hard muscles of his chest.

He lifted her face. "Maybe you should talk to him now. It could be important."

The cell phone rang again. She knew it could be important. But so was Dylan. "I won't do that to you."

"I'm a big boy," he said. "Take the call, sweetheart."

The unexpected endearment made her heart twist. "I don't want to," she whispered.

"I'm glad," he said, kissing her. Then he flipped open the phone. "What do you want, Jacobs?"

"Is, uh, Charlotte there?"

Charlotte heard Steve stumbling over the words and she took the phone from Dylan. "Hi, Steve."

"Oh, hi, Charlotte." She heard the relief in his voice. "Did I interrupt you?"

Dylan muffled a laugh against her hair. "What do you need?"

"To talk to you." He cleared his throat. "About what happened Saturday night."

She sat up. She felt self-conscious, sitting next to Dylan stark naked when he was fully clothed. He must have read her mind, because he draped her shirt over her shoulders.

Throwing Dylan a grateful look, she said to Steve, "Okay. How about this evening?"

"Um, I was kind of hoping that we could get together now. I need advice."

Dylan nodded. He handed her the rest of her clothes, then turned around. Her gaze lingered on him as she said, "All right. Meet me at the boat."

Snapping the phone closed, she stood and went to Dylan. Wrapping her arms around him from behind, she said, "You shouldn't have answered the phone."

"Steve needs you. And I should get back to Hayley."

"I'm sorry," she said.

"Don't be. I'm the one who answered the phone."

She dressed slowly, trying to ignore the loneliness she suddenly felt. The phone call was a reminder that she and Dylan lived in different worlds. Hers was here in Sturgeon Falls. His was with his daughter in Green Bay.

"Hey." He held her shoulders. "Don't look like that, or you'll make me think I wasn't very convincing. That you still think there's something wrong with you."

"Why did you answer the phone?"

"You think it was because I didn't want what you were offering?"

"It doesn't matter now, does it?"

"Charlotte, you definitely need more lessons. And I can't wait to give them to you." He pulled her close and kissed her.

"When?" she asked against his mouth.

"As soon as possible," he murmured. "Tomorrow?"

"Not tonight?"

"I promised Hayley we'd go to a movie and then miniature golfing. How about coming with us?"

"Hayley needs some time with just you. But I'm taking out a charter of two people tomorrow afternoon. Would you like to bring Hayley and come with me?"

"She'd love that. And so would I."

"Great." She walked out the door, waited for Dylan to join her, then locked it behind them. "I'll see you then."

He brushed a kiss over her mouth. "Think of me."

She watched as he ran down the steps. "I will."

CHAPTER TWELVE

STEVE WAS PERCHED on the side of her boat, tossing pebbles into the water. "Hey, Steve," she said as she stepped on board.

He turned around. "Sorry, Charlotte. I know you were with Mr. Smith." He threw another pebble into the water, harder. "Why didn't you tell me to get lost?"

Her face was slightly tender, and she suspected that it was red from whisker burn. Pressing her cool hands against her cheeks, she thought of the smile on Dylan's face when he'd left her. "It's okay, Steve. I told you to call anytime." Unlocking the cabin, she went in and sat on the couch. "What's up?"

He followed her in and flopped down beside her. Out of the sun, she could see that his eyes were red. "My father threw me out of the house." His hand shook as he pushed his hair out of his face. "He told me not to come back."

"Oh, Steve, I'm sorry." She reached over and grasped his hand. "Is there anything I can do to help?"

Steve's gaze hardened. "No. There's nothing you can do. Stay away from him, Charlotte. Don't even think about trying to talk to him. I don't want you to get hurt."

"He wouldn't hurt me." Steve's father was too much of a coward to go after anyone who would fight back. "But what about you? Do you have a place to stay?"

He shrugged. "I can stay with one of my buddies." He looked away, but not before she'd seen his uncertainty.

"You can stay here, if you'd like," she told him. "Until you get things straightened out."

"Yeah?"

"Of course." She couldn't bear to think of Steve wandering from one friend's house to another, feeling more lost and alone every day. "I'm sure it won't be long."

"He's not going to let me back in the house," Steve said bitterly.

Charlotte curled her legs beneath her and watched Steve. "Why don't you tell me what happened?"

Steve jumped to his feet and prowled the small space. "The sheriff called," he finally said. "My mother answered the phone. He wanted to make sure everything was okay—that I was okay." Steve shoved at a plastic chair across from the couch and it tumbled over. "He told her he wouldn't have arrested me if he'd been on duty. He would have brought me home, instead. God forbid the public works commissioner should be embarrassed by something his son did."

"Sheriff Godfrey was just following up, making sure you were all right," Charlotte said. "That's all."

"Come on, Charlotte." Steve turned to stare at her, and he looked far older than twenty-two. "You know the sheriff looks the other way when my father's involved. He's powerful around here. He controls a lot of jobs. Godfrey wanted to make sure Dad wasn't angry."

Charlotte wished Steve was wrong, but she knew he was right. The sheriff had been making excuses for Lyle Jacobs for years. "What happened after the sheriff called?"

"My father heard the end of the conversation. My mother wouldn't tell him who it was, said it was just a phone solicitor. So he checked the caller ID. When he saw that it was the sheriff, he called him back."

"And then what happened?" Charlotte asked, but she already knew. The hardness in Steve's expression, his clenched jaw, told the story.

"He hit my mother. In front of me. He hasn't done that in a long time."

Steve was still living at home to protect his mother, who refused to leave. "I'm sorry, Steve."

"Not as sorry as that son of a bitch is going to be. I punched him and knocked him down. I told him never to touch Mom again, or I'd kill him."

"And that's when he threw you out of the house."

"Yeah." Steve looked away. "I wanted Mom to come with me, but Dad said he'd kill her if she did. So I grabbed a few things and took off. I'm going to go back when I know he's gone and try to get her to leave."

"Did you call the sheriff?"

"Why bother?" he said bitterly. "She won't press charges. And I can't. He hasn't hit me since I called the sheriff that time when I was seventeen."

"The police have to arrest abusers, even if the victim won't press charges," Charlotte said. "Call them."

Steve shook his head. "It's my word against his. Guess whose word they're going to take."

Charlotte got up and picked up the chair. "You're right. I know you're right. But I want to do something."

"Letting me stay on your boat is huge," he said. "I don't want to tell my friends my dad kicked me out."

Of course he didn't. No young man wanted to admit to being humiliated and treated like a child. "You know you can't fix them," she said. "You can't make him stop hitting her, and you can't make her leave."

"Why not, damn it?" He slammed his fist against the wall and the boat shuddered. "Why does she let him hit her?"

Charlotte put her hand on Steve's shoulder. "You know it's not your fault and you know you can't force her to change," she said firmly. "Remember?"

"Don't give me that therapy crap."

"Then stop feeling sorry for yourself and do something." She forced him to face her. "You need to take care of yourself, Steve," she said, holding him more tightly when he tried to pull away. "You need to get your own head on straight before you can help your mom. Will you let me make an appointment for you with that therapist I know?"

"I already told you that I don't have any money to pay for that stuff," he muttered.

"He has a sliding scale for people who can't pay his full rates," she answered. "And I'll pay the difference."

"Why, Charlotte?" He raised his head, his gaze challenging. "Why would you do that for me?"

"I think this is more than you can handle on your own." She squeezed his shoulders then let him go. "Dr. Jantzen helped me a lot."

"I'll think about it." He kicked the wall and then looked at her apologetically. "He's going to want me to go to that AA crap, isn't he?"

"Probably."

"Everyone has a few beers now and then."

"Everyone doesn't get arrested for fighting when they drink," she retorted. "Everyone doesn't lose control of themselves when they have a few beers."

"I can control myself just fine. I can stop drinking anytime I want."

Painfully familiar words. Charlotte had heard them too often when she was growing up. "It's hard to admit you have a problem. And it's hard to do something about it," she said. "But you're strong, Steve. You can do it."

"The only problem I have is my father," he muttered.

"Will you at least give Dr. Jantzen a call and set up an appointment?"

"If I have to."

"I'm not going to make you call him," she answered. Steve had been forced into too many corners in his life. "It's your decision."

"I'll think about it."

"Fine." She glanced at her watch. "Are you ready for our charter this afternoon?"

"Of course." He tensed. "Unless you want Mr. Smith to do it?"

She wanted a lot of things from Dylan, but she didn't want to give him Steve's job. "I want you to do it, Steve. If you're up to it."

He nudged at a chair with his foot. "It's not like I have a broken arm or something. I can still steer the boat."

"Good," she said, smiling. "Then let's get things ready. They'll be here in less than an hour."

THE NEXT AFTERNOON, as Charlotte was getting the boat ready for yet another charter, she said to Steve, "There are going to be four on this trip."

"Four?" He stopped what he was doing, surprised. "There were only two names on the book."

"I invited two more people. Dylan and his daughter. She wanted to see what a fishing charter is all about." Charlotte fiddled with one of the fishing poles. She'd invited them impulsively and had spent the night wondering if she'd made a mistake. The interlude with Dylan on the couch the previous afternoon changed everything. How was she supposed to act toward Hayley? She'd had sex with the girl's father, for heaven's sake. This was getting too complicated.

"You're bringing him?"

She turned around when she heard the panic is his voice. "Is that a problem?"

"Did you tell him about me?" he demanded.

"The only thing he knows is that you're my first mate. And that you were arrested for fighting the other night. I wouldn't betray your confidence."

His shoulders relaxed. "Okay. But will it be all right with the people who booked the charter?"

"I already called them. They're thrilled that they'll only have to pay half as much."

"Right. I'll get a couple more poles."

As he clattered down the stairs to the closet, she spotted Dylan and Hayley on the pier. Hayley was kicking a stone from wooden slat to wooden slat, scowling. Dylan wore a matching scowl.

Great. Family tension. Just what she needed when she was already nervous. Had Dylan forced Hayley to come along? Did she have other plans? Charlotte tightened her grip on the cooler before putting it down, then straightened. "Hi," she said, moving toward them. "I'm so glad you could come with us, Hayley."

The girl raised one shoulder. "It'd be more fun without *him*." She glared at her father.

She glanced from Hayley's angry face to Dylan's clenched jaw and wondered desperately what to say. "No, it wouldn't," she finally answered with a bright smile. "Your dad is lots of fun on a fishing trip. He went out with me the other day and was a huge help."

"He's a jerk and I hate him."

"Oh, no. That's too bad. You know what we do with jerks on a boat, don't you?" she replied.

Hayley eyed her suspiciously. "What?"

"We make them walk the plank."

"You do not." But Hayley looked uncertain.

Dylan, Charlotte saw, had relaxed and he was almost smiling.

"Sure we do. But we have to wait until we're out on the lake. Until it's too far for them to swim to shore."

Hayley stared at her, then she hunched her shoulders. "Maybe he's not that big of a jerk."

"For small jerks, we make them scrub the deck," Charlotte said, smiling.

Hayley scowled. "Yeah. Make him scrub the deck."

"What did he do to deserve that?"

Hayley threw herself onto the cooler. "He treats me like a baby. Like I was about two years old."

"How so?"

"I asked for one little thing and he wouldn't let me do it. My mom would let me." She darted a challenging look at her father, who sighed.

"What did you ask him for?" Charlotte asked.

Hayley hunched her shoulders. "I want to get my belly button pierced."

"Ouch! That sounds really painful." Charlotte grabbed her stomach. "Why would you want to do that?"

Hayley raised her chin. "I want to wear those cool rings with diamonds and rubies and stuff in them."

Dylan, who was watching Hayley, shook his head. "Not going to happen, sugarplum."

"Don't call me that." She jumped up. "That's a baby name."

Dylan threw his hands into the air. "I beg your pardon, your highness."

Hayley's face got red. Time to divert attention. "Why do you want to wear a belly button ring?" Charlotte asked quickly.

"Because it looks so cool! I see girls with them at the mall all the time."

"Girls your age?"

Hayley lifted one shoulder. "Sure."

Translation—no. "You wear mostly T-shirts, don't you?" Charlotte had never seen her in anything else.

"Yeah."

"So no one could even see it."

"I'd know."

"I've heard those specific piercings are hard to take care of," Charlotte said, scrambling to remember what she'd read in a magazine a while ago. "That they get infected a lot. And bloody."

"I'm old enough to take care of it." She put her hands on her hips. "Or do you think I'm a baby, too?"

"I think you're very mature for your age." She hoped Dylan would jump in, but he looked as helpless as she felt. She brushed a wisp of hair away from her face and caught the edge of the stud she wore in her ear. Grasping at straws, she said, "Maybe you should try something a little simpler first."

"Like what?" Hayley asked, sneering. "Painting my toenails?"

What had happened to the pleasant child she'd met a few nights ago? "Maybe you could start out getting your ears pierced."

"Pierced ears are lame."

"Really?" Charlotte touched her own ears. "Maybe I should get a nose ring, then. Of course, that could be a problem when I had to blow my nose." She didn't look at Dylan, whose muffled snort of laughter made her bite her lip to keep from smiling.

Hayley recoiled. "That's gross."

"Okay, no nose ring. So what about getting your ears pierced?"

"He probably wouldn't let me get that done, either," Hayley muttered, shooting her father a dark look. Dylan sucked in his cheeks and tried to appear stern, but Charlotte saw his eyes twinkle.

"Have you asked him?"

"I know what he would say."

"Maybe he'd surprise you," she said lightly. Charlotte spotted a couple coming down the pier. "Here are my other guests. Think about it, Hayley." She glanced at Dylan for guidance. He gave her a tiny nod. "If your dad says yes and it's okay with your mom, I could take you downtown to get it done. There's a shop that does piercings there."

"Yeah?" Hayley's eyes lit up. "I'm not going to get my hopes up."

Smiling, Charlotte turned to the young couple

who'd reached her boat. "You must be the Dreyfusses," she said. "I'm Charlotte Burns. Come aboard."

An hour into the trip, Hayley was standing at the rear of the boat, watching Cecelia Dreyfuss reel in a salmon. "Can I net him, Charlotte?" she said excitedly. "I saw how you did the last one."

"Sure, but I'll help you. They can be tricky."

Charlotte waited for Cecelia to maneuver the fish to the boat, then she handed Hayley the net. Keeping a grip on the handle, she guided the girl as she scooped up the fish and then swung it into the boat. The fish flew out of the net, its silver scales glittering in the sunlight as it flopped on the deck.

"I did it!" Hayley turned to her father. "Did you see that, Dad? I netted the fish for Mrs. Dreyfuss."

"Good job," Dylan said, squeezing his daughter's shoulder. "You handled that like a pro."

"I'm going to be a fishing guide like Charlotte when I grow up." A grin split Hayley's face.

Bemused, Charlotte tossed the fish into the cooler. Just an hour ago Hayley had been sulking and unhappy. Now she was acting like she was on top of the world.

Dylan moved behind her. He was careful not to touch her, but Charlotte's nerves jumped. "One of the first things you learn about being a parent," Dylan said in a low voice. "They get over it a lot more quickly than you do."

"It's amazing." She watched Hayley, leaning over the side of the boat, throwing a piece of bread at a seagull. "Dr. Jekyll and Mr. Hyde."

Before he could answer, there was a hit on another line. "Who's next?" she said.

Four hours later they had a cooler full of salmon as they docked at the marina. Charlotte helped Steve lift it onto the pier, and the Dreyfusses followed him as he carried it toward the marina.

"Dad, can I watch Steve fillet the fish?" Hayley asked.

"Sure," he said. "Just don't go anywhere else. And when he's finished, come back here."

"Okay," she said as she ran down the pier.

Dylan waited until she was out of sight before saying to Charlotte, "Thank you for handling her so well. And if I have a vote, I say no nose ring for you." He touched her nose. "For what it's worth, I don't think you're lame."

She bent to secure a fishing pole. "I'm so relieved," she said breezily. "Being lame is my worst fear." She paused. "I'm sorry if I created a problem, suggesting that she get her ears pierced instead of her belly button."

"You didn't. I would have suggested it myself if she hadn't been so snotty about the belly button ring."

"Are you sure it will be okay with her mom?"

"I think so." He shook his head. "She's growing up so fast."

"I was surprised when she said you were a jerk and that she hated you. I thought you and Hayley had a strong relationship."

Dylan snorted. "We do, but I get that about once

a day. I try not to let it get to me, but it's tough sometimes. Hormones, Annie tells me."

He dropped his palms from her shoulders to her hands. "You were great with her, though. You knew just what to say."

"I was pretty much improvising."

"You're good at it," he murmured. He leaned closer. "And you're a great fishing guide. Are you good at everything you do?"

Her pulse jumped. "I don't know. There's a lot of stuff I haven't tried."

"Yeah? What kind of stuff?"

Her body humming, she took a step closer to Dylan. "Personal stuff," she said, breathless.

"Anything you need help with?" He trailed a finger down her cheek, down her neck, down her chest.

"Maybe." She couldn't catch her breath and she grabbed his hand before it could travel anywhere else.

"I'm up for anything, Charlotte," he whispered, cupping her face in his hands. "Anytime. Anywhere. Tonight?"

"Yes," she whispered back.

He bent closer and touched his mouth to hers, and she melted into him. She craved the feel of his body against hers, the taste of the coffee he'd been drinking, the scent of fresh air that clung to him. As she lost herself in his kiss, she wrapped her arms around him and pulled him close.

"What's going on?"

Hayley's voice shattered the spell, and Charlotte jerked away from Dylan. Hayley stood on the pier, her mouth quivering. "You lied to me! You said she wasn't your girlfriend."

CHAPTER THIRTEEN

"Is THAT WHY YOU brought me here?" Hayley stared at her father, betrayal a sick feeling in her stomach. "So you could be with her?"

"I invited you," Charlotte said, stepping away from her dad. "You said you wanted to see what a fishing trip would be like. I only had two people for this trip, so it seemed like a good time for you to come along."

"You're lying! You just wanted my dad. You didn't want me."

"You're wrong, Hayley." Charlotte sounded so calm. Like there was nothing wrong. Like she hadn't just been swapping spit with Hayley's dad. "I loved showing you my boat the other night. I enjoyed how excited you were about it. You reminded me of myself at your age."

She didn't want to listen to Charlotte. She'd thought the woman was cool. She had planned on asking her dad if she could get a pair of water sandals like the ones Charlotte wore. She was even going to grow her hair long enough to pull it into a ponytail.

Her mouth quivered. "I hate you!" she yelled. She looked at her father through suddenly blurry eyes. "And I hate you, too." When he started toward her, she turned and ran down the pier. Her footsteps sounded hollow as they echoed over the water.

Her dad caught up with her before she reached the car. "Hold on, Hayley."

He tried to take her hand but she jerked away from him. "Leave me alone."

"Stop it," he said, and he had that tone in his voice. That tone that said she'd better listen. She reluctantly stopped.

"Why did you lie to me?" she cried, her chest tight. "Why did you tell me she wasn't your girlfriend?"

"When you asked, she wasn't," he answered calmly. "She was a source for a story. That's all."

"That was just a few days ago." She sneered. "Give me a break."

"A lot can happen in a few days," he said, getting a weird smile on his face. That smile made her chest feel even tighter.

"You don't even like boats. So why are you hanging around with her?"

"I'm hanging around with Charlotte. Not her boat."

"I suppose you're going to move here to be with her," she said, trying to sound as if she didn't care.

"Of course not. What gave you an idea like that?" He reached out for her, but she ducked to avoid him.

"She's your girlfriend. I know what that means. It means you're going to spend all your time with her."

"You're wrong," he said, turning her to face him. "I'm going to spend as much time with you as I ever did. Any time I spend with Charlotte is separate from that."

"I don't believe you."

"Why not? Have I ever lied to you?" He put his finger beneath her chin and lifted her head so she had to look at him.

She jerked her head away. "Mom was on a date last night," she said, kicking at a stone. "That's why she called me so late."

"Is that what this is about?" He tried to pull her into his arms, but she resisted. "Your mom was on a date, then you see me kissing Charlotte, and you're afraid we're going to leave you?"

"Some of my friends' fathers have girlfriends," she muttered. "They're never around."

"Hayley." He grabbed her hands. She wanted to get away from him, but she found herself holding on to him. "Look at me." He waited. "Nothing will change the way I feel about you, or the way your mom feels about you. Nothing. You're our daughter. We love you, and you'll always be the most important person in the world for both of us. But sometimes we want to be with other adults. Sometimes we want to go on dates. That doesn't mean we love you any less."

"Are you having sex with her?"

His grip tightened, then he dropped her hands. He looked sad. As if she'd let him down. She hated that look. It always made her squirm inside.

"That's a rude question, Hayley. My relationship with Charlotte is private. It's between me and Charlotte and no one else."

"That means yes, doesn't it?"

"It means it's none of your business. And I think you owe Charlotte an apology."

"For what? I didn't say anything wrong." She stuck her chin out at him, but she was cringing inside. She was afraid that if she said anything to Charlotte, she'd cry. And only babies cried.

Her dad looked disappointed. Then he pulled the keys out of his pocket. "Go wait in the car. I'm going to apologize to Charlotte for your behavior. Then we'll talk."

She swallowed around the huge lump in her throat as she walked away. When she reached the end of the pier, she turned around. He was still watching, and he lifted a hand and waved.

Spinning around, she stomped to the car, yanked open the door and threw herself on the seat.

Dylan walked back to Charlotte's boat. She was stowing the fishing rods in the cabin.

"How is she?" Charlotte asked.

"About like you'd expect a jealous twelve-year-old to be." He sighed and shoved his hand through his hair. "I haven't had many, uh, girlfriends since Annie and I divorced," he said. "I've mostly dated casually." For sex, with a willing partner and the understanding there were no strings attached. "So she's not used to seeing me with women. It was a shock. I'm really sorry."

"Don't worry about it. I understand." She sighed. "At least we weren't doing anything really inappropriate."

In another few seconds they would have been. God. Why did Charlotte make him lose all sense of control? "I need to spend some time with her. So tonight is out."

"I know. It's okay," she said. She kissed him, nothing more than a brush of lips. Even so, it made him reach for her. But she moved away before he could touch her.

"Take care of Hayley," she said. "Reassure her. Make sure she knows how much you love her." Her smile was wistful. "She's so lucky to have you."

"What are you going to do this evening?"

She propped herself against the side of the boat. "Absolutely nothing besides eat something and fall into bed."

He debated asking her if he could see her later, after Hayley was asleep. No. Tonight had to be for Hayley. "Think of me." He pressed a kiss to her lips and quickly stepped away, before he could change his mind.

THE NEXT MORNING, Charlotte was sitting in a chair on the deck of Gus's boat, watching him tie lures. His fingers moved slowly, and he didn't try to tie the smaller ones, but he still made his own lures. "You want some help with those?" she asked, sipping her coffee.

"I can tie my own lures," he said without looking up. "You think I'm too old to do it? Or maybe I can't see well enough?" He dropped the completed holly fly into his tackle box, then flexed his fingers a few times.

He didn't realize she knew about the arthritis in his hands.

"You still tie the best lures I've seen," she said, stretching her legs out in the sun. "But you always told me many hands make the work light."

"You've been talking to that daughter of mine, haven't you?" He defiantly picked up a hook and started another lure.

"I talk to Kat all the time."

"You know what I mean. She told you, didn't she?"

"Yes, Gus, she did." Setting her coffee down, she put her hands over his. "You don't have to do everything yourself. I want to help you."

Gus set the hook on the table. "I know you do, Charlotte. You're a good girl. I promise, when it's too hard to make the lures, I'll let you do it."

"Okay." That was as much of a concession as she was going to get, and she knew it. She'd let it go for now, but she decided that a few of her lures would find their way into Gus's tackle box.

She heard footsteps on the pier behind her. "Hi, Charlotte. Mr. Macauley."

Dylan. She turned around, trying to not leap to her feet to greet him. "Hi, Dylan. Hayley." The girl stood next to Dylan, clearly uncomfortable. "Were you guys looking for me?"

Dylan nodded. "Hayley has something she needs to say."

"I'm sorry, Charlotte," the girl said in a small voice. "I was snotty and mean to you yesterday. I won't do it again."

"Thank you, Hayley," Charlotte said. "You're forgiven. Come aboard and meet a friend of mine."

Hayley glanced at Dylan, and he nodded once. The two of them must have straightened things out last night. The girl stepped onto the boat, followed by Dylan.

He brushed against her arm as he reached to shake Gus's hand, and Charlotte shivered. When he brushed by her again, she leaned into him.

"Good morning, Mr. Macauley," Dylan said. "Do you remember my daughter, Hayley? You met at the fish boil."

Gus shook hands with Hayley. "Of course I remember you. And call me Gus, both of you," he said gruffly. His gaze lingered on Hayley. "Charlotte tells me you caught a salmon yesterday."

"I did." Hayley began chattering to Gus about that fish and the one she'd helped net. "I'm going to be a charter captain, too," she said.

"Yeah?" Gus sat back and watched her. "It's a tough job."

"I can do it. I'm tough."

Gus laughed. "I can see that," he said. "Do you want to look around my boat?"

"Can I?"

"As long as your dad says it's okay."

"It's fine," Dylan said. "Just don't touch Mr. Macauley's stuff."

"I won't."

She scrambled into the cabin, and Gus looked at Dylan. "Nice kid," he said. "She reminds me of Charlotte."

"I was the toughest kid around," Charlotte said lightly.

"I hated that you had to be," he said.

She could feel Dylan looking at her. "But thanks to you and Frances, I grew up perfect, right?" she said, forcing a grin.

"I don't know about perfect," Gus said. "You've got an ornery streak a mile wide."

Smiling to herself, she steered the conversation toward safer waters. Gus might know how to push her buttons, but she knew how to push his, as well.

Dylan sat next to her on the bench, close enough that their legs touched. "How are you feeling, Gus?" he asked.

"Great. Never better." He didn't meet Charlotte's gaze. "I have a charter booked for the first part of next week."

"It must be a relief to get back to work," Dylan said.

"It sure is. I've had about enough of women hovering over me," he said.

"You big phony," Charlotte said, shaking her head. "You've had three women catering to you. You love it."

"I need to get back to work," he said quietly, and Charlotte reached across the table to squeeze his hand.

"I know," she said. "But you have to ease into it."

He sighed. "Like you and Frances and Kat would let me do anything else. At least Frances is letting

171

me run some errands again. I have to stop by Tilda's Garden on my way home to pick up her flowers."

"Make sure one of the clerks loads them into your truck for you," she said.

"I'm perfectly capable of lifting a flat of flowers. Back off, Charlotte."

"How are things going with those developers who want to buy the marina?" Dylan interjected smoothly.

Charlotte acknowledged his intervention with a smile. "I haven't seen or heard from any of them for a while," she said. "Maybe they changed their minds."

"They didn't," Gus said. "Two came to see me the other day. Different ones."

"What did they have to say?"

"Same old stuff as the last guys. But it sounded like they were threatening me. I tossed them out of the house."

"They came to your house?" Charlotte sat up straight. "I don't like that."

Gus shrugged. "My address is no secret."

"And they threatened you?" Dylan asked. "What did they look like?"

Gus frowned. "Younger. Suits. They were real smooth."

Dylan pulled his notebook out of his pocket. "Can you be more specific? Color of their hair, their eyes, the shape of their face, that kind of thing?"

"One of them had dark brown hair. The other one was lighter. Both cut short. The first guy was tall and rangy. The other one was short and stocky."

Dylan glanced over at her, wary. "Sounds like it could be the two from your boat trip."

"Maybe. That's pretty vague, though." She tried to be nonchalant, but apprehension seized her. "Why did you think they were threatening you?"

"Bastards," he growled. "They said I was getting up there in years. Asked me how many more years I planned to work, what would my wife do if something happened to me and I couldn't work anymore. Said I should think about taking their money while I could."

"That does sound threatening," she said.

"No way to prove it, though." Dylan snapped his notebook shut and stuffed it in his pocket. "If you challenged them, they'd say they were talking about your recent illness. They were smooth, all right." He studied Gus. "Maybe you should back off and let someone else take point on this marina thing."

"Are you saying I'm not up to negotiating with them?" He thrust out his jaw.

"Of course not. All I'm saying is let someone else handle the negotiations."

Good luck, Charlotte thought. She wanted Gus out of the loop, as well. But she wasn't holding her breath.

"I haven't backed down from a fight yet, and I'm not about to start," Gus answered. "Forget it. I can tell them no as well as anyone."

"What about selling out at this marina and going somewhere else? Avoid the stress altogether."

"Hell, no. This is where I've worked from for the past twenty-five years. A couple of punks aren't going to scare me into selling."

"You could get a nice piece of change and keep doing your charters."

"And let them win? Not going to happen." He cocked his head. "Are you working for them, Smith?"

"Of course not."

"No one is chasing me from this marina. You're a city boy. Spend your time behind a desk. You don't understand my life. Or Charlotte's, for that matter. So don't try to tell me what to do."

"I wasn't trying to tell you anything." Dylan's voice was mild, but Charlotte could hear his irritation. "I thought we were having a conversation."

"Not if you're going to nag me about selling." Gus stood up and pushed his chair back. "I'm going to show that little girl around my boat."

Charlotte watched Gus stomp into the cabin. In a few moments, they heard his gruff voice and Hayley's higher-pitched one. She glanced over at Dylan, who was listening, bemused.

"Is he always this much of a grouch?" Dylan asked.

"He's been hearing the same thing from me and Kat and Frances," she said. "So he's touchy on the subject. Maybe he overreacted."

Dylan snorted. "Ya think?"

Charlotte nodded toward the door. "He's not being grouchy with Hayley."

She could see through the open door that he'd pulled out his charts and topological maps to show Hayley the best fishing areas.

Dylan took her hand. "It sounds as if Gus has himself a new convert."

She was stabbed by a completely unexpected shard of jealousy. She remembered clearly the first time she'd been on this boat, enthralled and excited, and he'd pulled out his charts and told her how to use them to catch fish.

How pathetic was that, to be jealous of a child. She didn't own Gus. She should be happy that Hayley had taken his mind off his illness and the mess with the developers.

But suddenly Charlotte knew exactly how Hayley had felt yesterday when she'd seen her father kissing Charlotte. Suddenly, Charlotte was twelve years old again, watching her friend Kat and her parents, longing for something she would never have.

Feeling alone and outside the circle.

CHAPTER FOURTEEN

"YEAH, GUS LOVES introducing kids to fishing." In the cabin, Charlotte saw Hayley's head of dark red hair bent close to Gus's, heard the low murmur of their voices. "Enjoy your visit with him," she added to Dylan.

She stuck her head in the door. "I have to go," she said to Gus. "Do you want me to grab those flowers for Frances and drop them off at your house?"

"What?" Gus said, distracted. "Flowers?"

"The ones that Frances wanted."

He glanced at the girl sitting next to him. "Sure," he said. "Hayley and I need more time to study these charts."

Hayley grinned at him. "I already know about fishing. From yesterday."

"Charlotte's good," Gus acknowledged. "But she learned everything she knows from me."

"She did?" Hayley's eyes grew wide.

"She was my first mate." He nodded. "You look like a fast learner. Just like Charlotte."

Charlotte couldn't read Hayley's reaction.

She was a complete idiot. It must be lack of sleep.

She watched Gus and Hayley, her eyes blurring, then she turned blindly and jumped onto the pier.

"You're not going to stick around?" Dylan asked, following her.

She shook her head. "I'm going to pick up those flowers for Frances and save Gus a trip." And get away from the marina for a while.

"You're leaving me alone with Gus?" His eyebrows rose. "Without you to protect him?"

She smiled. "I think Gus can take it," she said. "You're not that bad."

"Wow. Coming from you, that's high praise." His voice was teasing, but she saw understanding in his eyes.

"You look like you want to go with her, Smith."

Gus's voice startled her. She hadn't realized he was watching them. "Go ahead," he said. "Hayley and I are going to take the downriggers apart and clean them. We'll be busy for a while."

Was Gus playing matchmaker? She was afraid what Hayley might think.

"Is that okay with you, honey?" Dylan asked the child. "Or do you want me to stay here with you and Gus?"

"Of course not." Hayley couldn't take her eyes off Gus. "I want Gus to show me how to take care of the downriggers. We don't need you to help us."

Dylan shook his head, murmuring to Charlotte, "Another man has taken my place. Is this how fathers feel when their daughters get married?" He added to Hayley, "I'll be back soon. Do you have your phone?"

She patted her pocket. "Right here."

"See you in a while."

Charlotte headed for the parking lot. "You don't have to come with me," she said. "You can stay with Hayley."

He scoffed. "I'd just be in the way. You saw how she was looking at Gus."

The same way *she* used to look at Gus. Like he was the center of the universe. "He'll take good care of her."

"What's wrong, Charlotte?" he asked quietly.

"Nothing." She hoped the look she gave him was appropriately bewildered. "Why would there be something wrong?"

He smoothed his hand over her hair. "You seemed sad on the boat."

She shrugged, but he persisted. "I know something's wrong. I know you, Charlotte."

"It's nothing. It's stupid and petty."

"It's Hayley and Gus, isn't it? It feels like she's taking your place."

"I told you it was stupid and petty."

"It's neither. It's like seeing your father cooing over the new baby."

"Okay, let's add childish to the list."

He touched her face, let his fingers trail down her arm. "It's a compliment," he said gently. "He's reliving the time when you were Hayley's age and so eager to learn. Because it meant so much to him."

Speechless, she stared at him. "You keep surprising me," she finally said.

"Good. I want to keep you off balance."

"You're succeeding."

"I owe Gus. I've been trying to get you alone since the afternoon at your house. And he just dropped you into my hands."

"We'll hardly be alone," she said, regretting that she'd promised to go to Tilda's Garden.

"You don't think so? I'm very resourceful, Charlotte. Especially when I want something. And I want you. A lot."

Her skin prickled and she caught her breath. "You can't leave Hayley here that long."

"I can leave her for a while. Long enough to steal a kiss from you. She basically told me to get lost."

"You'd better be careful." She took a deep breath, trying to steady her heart rate. "By the time you get back, Hayley is going to want a boat of her own."

"She could do worse," he said, tugging her closer. "You turned out pretty well."

"Being a charter boat captain isn't want most people want for their daughters. It's hard work, physically and mentally. And there are no guarantees."

"Parents want their kids to be happy. They want them to find their passion, what they love to do." He smiled. "But she's only twelve. Chances are, there will be a lot of things she wants to do before she's an adult."

"That's very enlightened."

"What can I say? I'm an enlightened guy." He brushed a lock of hair away from her face. "Who loves his daughter and wants her to be happy."

"You're a good father, Dylan."

He raised their joined hands and kissed her fingers. "Let me guess," he said. "Your mother didn't want you to have a boat."

She remembered the fights they'd had after she became Gus's first mate. "She thought I should be a doctor, like Kat." There was more money in medicine.

"You said you hated the idea of being stuck inside a hospital all day."

She was surprised and pleased that he'd remembered. "I did. But my mom didn't think that should stop me."

Opening the door to her truck, she said, "Last chance to back out. I have to get the flowers for Frances. You could get a cup of coffee and read the newspaper instead."

"Only if you're having coffee and reading the paper with me." He lounged against the truck. "I don't care what we do, Charlotte. I just want to spend time with you."

"Okay, then." She climbed into the truck and waited for him, then started the engine. "You really are Mr. Smooth, aren't you?"

"Not anymore." He shifted on the seat. "Half the time I feel like some awkward, geeky teenager around you."

"What about the other half?" she managed to say over the sudden pounding of her heart.

"The other half?" He trailed one finger down her cheek, over her lips. "I want you so bad I can't remember my own name."

His words hung in the air, making her heart speed up and her chest tighten. She pushed too hard on the accelerator and the truck leaped forward, spitting gravel. "Why do you always leave me speechless? What am I supposed to say to that?"

"How about, 'I want you, too, Dylan'?"

"You know I do." She gripped the steering wheel more tightly. "I haven't made any secret of that."

"No." He tugged on her ponytail. "Are you going to take what you want?"

Yes. It was inevitable. She turned to putty when he put his hands on her. It was terrifying how easily he could strip away her control. "It's also not a secret that I don't want to get involved," she said, trying to get some of it back. "Especially with a guy who's leaving Sturgeon Falls."

"It's not like I live on the other side of the country. Green Bay is less than an hour away."

"You have ties in Green Bay. Your job. Your daughter. Your friends. You're not going to pick up and move here." She stopped, horrified. He'd never said anything about moving, about anything more serious than a vacation fling. Where had that come from?

From her, she realized in a panic. She was the one building daydreams about Dylan. "And besides, you don't do relationships. Remember?"

"You could make me change my mind." His voice was so soft that she wondered if she was imagining it. Hearing what she wanted to hear.

"We just met," she said. "This is crazy talk."

"Maybe that's because you make me crazy."

He made her crazy, too. And it scared her senseless.

"Here's Tilda's Garden," she said, both relieved and disappointed.

"Let's go find those flowers."

Crowds of people wandered through the nursery, some of them pulling red wagons full of flowers. Charlotte hurried toward the cash registers, pleased to see Amy Mitchell. "Hi, Amy. How are you doing?"

Amy smiled, her happiness obvious. "I'm great, Charlotte. How about you?"

"I'm good." Charlotte saw the sparkle of a diamond on Amy's finger. "You and George are engaged?" She gave Amy a hug. "That's wonderful. When are you getting married?"

"In October. As soon as things slow down here and George settles in with his students." Amy twisted the ring. "We didn't want to wait too long."

"I'm happy for you, Amy." And she was. After struggling as a single mother for over eight years, Amy deserved a man who loved her. But being happy for Amy didn't ease the loneliness that cut into her like a cold gust of wind.

"Did you talk to Frances Macauley?" she asked Amy. "She called about flats of flowers."

"Let me check." Amy grabbed an envelope next to the register and thumbed through some invoices. "Here it is. She wants two flats of snapdragons, two of impatiens and one of alyssum." She looked around. "Do you want me to get one of the kids to find them for you?"

"We can do it," Charlotte said, reaching for a wagon.

As they walked away from the registers, Dylan took the handle. "Let's check behind that shed," he said, heading toward a small building at the rear of the nursery. "That looks like a good spot."

"There aren't any flowers there."

He flashed a grin as he pulled her behind the shed. "I know."

As soon as they were out of sight, he backed her up against the building. The wood was warm against her back and Dylan's hands were hot on her face as he held her still for his kiss.

Charlotte wrapped her arms around him, pulled him close and kissed him. Dylan groaned into her mouth and dropped one hand down her side, pressing her hips closer to his. She clung to him, her hands roaming his back, need pouring through her.

Dylan slipped his hand beneath her shirt. As she moved against him, pressing her breast into his palm, she heard a sound.

"Oh, excuse me." A woman's voice, filled with amusement, made Charlotte freeze, but Dylan didn't move.

When he finally stepped away, the woman was gone. As Charlotte straightened her shirt, Dylan grinned.

"Oops."

"Oh, God. Let's get out of here," Charlotte said, feeling her face flame.

"In a minute, sweetheart." He bumped his hip

against her. "Let's give…things a chance to settle down."

She glanced down at the front of Dylan's shorts and touched her forehead to his. "I am so busted."

"Relax," he said, squeezing her hand. "She couldn't see you. All she could see was my back."

Please, God, let that be true. Otherwise, she'd never hear the end of it. In spite of the tourists, Sturgeon Falls was a very small town.

"Let's get the flowers and get out of here," she muttered.

"Good idea. Somewhere more private."

"We're not going to find it at Frances's house."

"After we drop the flowers off for Frances."

The air in the car was charged with tension as they drove to the Macauleys'. As she stopped at the curb, she said, "I'll see where Frances wants these."

"No problem."

Frances wanted them in the backyard, she said when she opened the door. Then she glared at Charlotte. "Why did he send you? Is he doing something on that boat he shouldn't be doing?"

"He's having a great time," Charlotte said over her shoulder as she headed for the truck. "He's showing Dylan's daughter the ropes. She says she wants to be a charter captain when she grows up."

Frances's expression hardened. "Dylan? That reporter?"

"Yes," she said, puzzled by the coldness in the other woman's voice. But before she could ask her why, Dylan stepped out of the truck.

"Where are we putting the flowers?" he said.

"In the backyard."

Frances didn't say anything as they carried the flats into her backyard. When they finished, Charlotte put her hand on Dylan's arm. "Would you mind waiting in the truck? There's something I need to talk to Frances about."

"Sure." He headed toward the truck, and Charlotte went into the house.

"What's going on?" she asked Frances. "What do you have against Dylan? For heaven's sake, you only met him once and he was perfectly pleasant."

"He's cocky. And arrogant. I don't like pushy men."

"How can you say that, Frances? You don't even know him. You exchanged a couple of words with him."

Frances sniffed. "I know what I know."

"No, you don't. You haven't given him a chance. I like him, Frances. A lot. I want to spend time with him."

"Why him?" Frances trembled. "He's an outsider, Charlotte. He's leaving."

"Maybe. But until he does, I'm going to see him. Don't make me choose between you," she said. "Don't hurt me that way."

Frances turned away, but not before Charlotte had seen the tears in her eyes. "I don't want to hurt you, Charlotte. Maybe your reporter *is* a good man. But he's asking questions about the orchard, digging up the past, and it hurts. All I want is to forget about the orchard."

Charlotte put her arm around Frances. "How come?"

"The time when Gus worked at the orchard was horrible for me. For us. We were having problems, and his questions bring back those bad memories. I just want to forget about that period in our lives, but it's hard to do that if he stirs things up."

Charlotte squeezed her tightly. "I know why Dylan is here. I can't break his confidence, but it has nothing to do with you or Gus. I promise you. Dylan needs some information and he thought Gus might be able to help him, since he worked at the orchard. That's all."

"He doesn't want to know about Gus?"

"Not at all. He wanted to talk to Gus because there aren't a lot of people around who worked there years ago."

Frances drew back to look at her. "Okay. I trust you, Charlotte. I'll let it go. I'll be nice to your young man."

"Thank you. That means a lot to me."

After kissing Frances goodbye, Charlotte got back in her truck. Dylan asked, "Is everything all right?"

"Everything's fine. Frances has been afraid you're going after Gus for some reason. The time he worked in the orchard was stressful for both of them." She sighed. "I guess it would be, if he didn't want to be there. I told her you only needed information."

"I'm sorry if my questions upset her."

"The past couple of months have been hard for her. She'd been helping Kat by taking care of Regan, and then she fell and broke her arm. She feels as though she let Kat down and she's frustrated by the cast. And then Gus got sick. It's been tough."

"Then I started asking questions about a bad time in her life. No wonder she didn't want anything to do with me. You've been trying to protect her. That's why you didn't want me to go to the fish boil the other night."

"Yes," she admitted. "I didn't want her to have to deal with anything else."

"You take good care of her."

"She takes better care of me," she replied. "Frances was more of a mother to me than my own mother."

"What's the story with your mom?"

She tried to dismiss the pain, but it was still there, lodged like a splinter in her heart. "Nothing that unusual. She was a single mother, she worked two jobs, and when she wasn't working, she was drowning her sorrows. She wasn't home a lot."

"Poor Charlotte."

"Don't feel sorry for me. I got all the attention I needed from Gus and Frances."

"Not the same."

"No." She gripped the steering wheel.

"Do you see her often?" he asked.

"Once in a while." She glanced at him out of the corner of her eye. "It's difficult, you know? To spend time with her. She doesn't approve of my lifestyle. And I don't approve of hers."

"Is she still drinking?"

"Last time I talked to her, she told me she'd stopped. Said she was going to AA meetings."

"You don't believe her?"

She sighed. "I hope it's true. But she's said that before."

"You should visit her. See for yourself." A shadow of pain crossed his face. "You never know how long you have with your parents."

"I know." It took a while to steel herself for another visit with her mother. For the weeping, the complaints and the anger. "I will."

He ran his hand through her hair and cupped the back of her neck. His hand felt steady and strong, and she wanted to lean against him for a while, to absorb some of his strength.

But his cell phone rang, and he eased away from her.

Charlotte could hear the conversation clearly.

"Daddy? Where are you?" Hayley's voice sounded petulant through the cell phone.

Just that fast, Dylan went from her lover to Hayley's father. And Charlotte was alone again.

CHAPTER FIFTEEN

"WE'RE RUNNING ERRANDS for Gus," Dylan said. "Are you having a good time with him?"

"Yeah, he's fun, but I wondered where you were."

Sighing, he glanced at Charlotte and mouthed, "How far?"

She held up five fingers.

"I'm five minutes away, baby. Okay?"

"Okay. I'll see you soon."

He snapped his phone closed. So much for more time with Charlotte.

"I have to get back to Hayley," he said. "She's getting restless."

"That's okay," she said. "We've been gone almost an hour, anyway."

"Yeah, Hayley can be high energy. Gus probably needs a break."

"That's not what I meant." She frowned. "Hayley is a great kid, but Gus always tries to do too much. He's probably trying to figure out how to get her on the water and put a fishing rod in her hand."

Wisps of hair from her ponytail curled around her face in the breeze from the open window, and her lips looked soft and tempting. He wanted to taste her again.

Not a good idea while driving down Michigan Street. Instead, he skimmed his hand over her cheek. Her skin was satin-smooth beneath his fingers.

She sighed when he touched her. He smoothed his thumb over her lips. "Can we get together this evening?" he murmured. "For dinner?"

She pressed her lips into his palm. "I'd like that," she said. "A lot."

Desire rushed through him, fueled by the passion in Charlotte's eyes. "Me, too. I'll pick you up at seven-thirty. Is that okay?"

"Seven-thirty it is." She sounded breathless, and his heart raced.

When they got to the marina, he took her hand. She bumped against him until they neared Gus's boat. Then she disentangled her hand and put some distance between them. "No sense throwing gasoline on the fire. Let Hayley get used to the idea of us together."

"Smart woman," he said. His daughter had never seen him kiss a woman other than his ex-wife before yesterday.

"Anyone home?" Charlotte called.

"We're inside," Gus replied.

Dylan followed Charlotte into the cabin, bumping into her when she stopped abruptly. Gus and Hayley sat at the galley table, their heads together. They were doing something with colored string.

"They're tying lures," Charlotte explained.

Hayley held up what looked like a little pom-

pom of blue and pink strings. "Look what I made, Dad," she said, her eyes shining. "It's a holly fly."

"Very cool, sweetheart," he said, enjoying her excitement. "What do you use it for?"

"To catch salmon, of course." She rolled her eyes.

"Ah." He slung an arm over Charlotte's shoulders. "Maybe Charlotte will take us fishing again so you can try it out."

Hayley watched Charlotte, standing in front of her dad. *Too close.* "I'm going to go out with Gus. Next week."

"You may not be here next week," her dad said gently.

Hayley frowned. "Why wouldn't I be here?"

"I haven't talked to your mom, so I'm not sure what the plan is. Okay?"

"Why can't I stay here, even if Aunt Joan is better? Gus promised he'd take me fishing."

Gus stood up. "Your dad and I will talk about our trip another time. Okay, Hayley?"

"Sure, Gus," she said. She set the lure carefully into Gus's case. "I'll see you later."

"Don't you want to take your holly fly?" Gus asked. His eyes crinkled. "Here you go."

She cupped it in her hand. The pink and blue threads stuck between her fingers, and she tightened her grip until the hook stung her hand. She wasn't going to use it to fish. She didn't want to get salmon spit all over it.

"I'll see you at seven-thirty," Charlotte said to her dad. Then she smiled at her and Gus and left.

Her dad was going out with Charlotte tonight?

"You can't go out with Charlotte," she said. "We were supposed to go bowling. Remember?"

"You're going bowling with Kendall and Gabe and Shelby and Jenna. I wasn't part of those plans."

"You have to come," she insisted. "I don't want to go alone."

Her dad gave her that squinty look that made her nervous. "Since when do I need to tag along when you go out with your friends?"

Since you want to go out with Charlotte. "They're not really my friends," she said. "We're just staying with them."

He nudged her toward the pier. "Let's go. We'll talk about this later. Gus probably has things he needs to do."

Yeah, and her dad needed to get ready for his date with Charlotte. "In a minute, Dad."

"Now, Hayley."

She scowled, but jumped off the boat. "Thanks, Gus, for showing her around the boat," her dad said.

"Anytime." Gus nodded at her.

As they were walking down the pier, Charlotte came up behind them. "Hold on, Hayley," she said. She handed her a clear plastic case divided into six sections. "For your holly fly," she said with a smile. "Every fisherman needs one for her lures."

It looked just like the box Hayley had seen Charlotte use. Staring at it, Hayley thought it was the coolest thing anyone had ever given her. She opened it carefully and set the lure in one of the sections. "Thank you," she said in a small voice.

"You're welcome, Hayley."

"It looks like you had a good time with Mr. Macauley," her dad said as they continued down the pier.

"He told me to call him Gus. We had a great time." She forgot about Charlotte as she told him about the downriggers and studying the charts and tying the lures.

Finally, when they got into the car, he said, "Why did you call me, then, baby? I rushed back here because I thought you were in a hurry to leave."

Guilt made her feel sick to her stomach, but she forced herself to shrug. "I just wondered where you were. I wanted to know what you were doing."

"Does Charlotte have something to do with this?"

She stared out the window. "I don't know why you had to go with her. You could have stayed with Gus and me."

"Did you need me there?" he asked. "Were you uncomfortable with Gus?"

"Of course not," she said impatiently. "Gus and I were talking about boats."

He started the car. "You seemed to be having a good time with Gus and Charlotte needed help with her errands. That's why I went with her."

"Yeah? I thought you wanted to kiss her some more."

"I thought we talked about the whole dating thing," he said cautiously.

She hunched one shoulder. "I guess."

"Has Charlotte been mean to you?"

"No."

"Then why don't you like her?"

"She's okay." Charlotte was nice, really. But her dad was different now, and Hayley didn't like it.

"Fine. You're entitled to your opinions."

She didn't want to talk about Charlotte. She opened the box and picked up her lure. "Isn't this the coolest thing ever?"

Her dad sighed. "Yeah, it is. Maybe when we get to the house you can show me how you made it."

CHARLOTTE SMOOTHED the sleeveless black dress down her thighs and looked in the mirror. The deep V neck clung to her curves and the hem barely skimmed her knees. As she studied the unfamiliar figure in the mirror, her face heated. She couldn't wear this tonight. Everyone who saw her would know exactly what she had planned.

Including Dylan.

Her hand hovered over the zipper, then she dropped it. Why couldn't she wear a sexy dress, feel feminine and pretty? Why couldn't she enjoy watching a man watch her?

Who cared what the other people at the restaurant thought? Tonight was for her. And Dylan.

Her hair fell in soft waves around her shoulders, and the seldom-used makeup made her look like a mysterious stranger. She turned away from the mirror.

She didn't care what anyone thought. She'd let that rat bastard Kyle Franklin mess with her mind for far too long. Tonight she was going to have fun with Dylan. And if they ended up at her house after dinner…she'd enjoy that, too.

She was ready way too early, so she sat on the couch and picked up the novel she'd been reading. But she couldn't concentrate on the story. In spite of her bravado, her leg bounced up and down and her heart matched its beat.

The phone rang and she jumped. "Hello?"

"Hi, Charlotte." Dylan.

"Hi," she said as she sank into the couch cushion. "How are you?"

"I've been better," he said. His voice sounded grim.

"What's wrong?" She bolted upright. "Are you okay?"

"I'm fine. It's Hayley."

"Oh, no. Is she sick? Hurt? Is there anything I can do?"

"Only if you can find me some patience. Hayley is going bowling with Kendall and Gabe and the girls tonight. But she's insisting that I come along."

Disappointment nearly crushed Charlotte, but she said, "We can have dinner another night."

"Damn it, Charlotte, don't be so understanding. Get angry with me for standing you up. Yell at me or something."

"She's your daughter, Dylan." Charlotte was still outside the circle. First with Gus, earlier today, and now Dylan. Her throat swelled.

He sighed. "She's manipulating me and I know

it. But she's confused and worried because suddenly both her mother and I are dating. That's why I let her get away with it. But I don't like it."

"We don't have to go out to dinner," she said slowly. "I can make dinner here. If you still want to get together."

"Of course I do." The desire in his voice burned through the telephone. "But it'll be nine o'clock before I can get away, and I know you probably have to be up early tomorrow."

"I'm not going to worry about tomorrow," she said, suddenly reckless. "I'll see you around nine."

"Are you sure?"

"I'm sure."

"Excellent. But don't make dinner. I'll bring carryout. I'll see you later."

Six-thirty. Dylan wouldn't be here for a while. She should change her dress, now that they weren't going out. Put on something more casual.

No. She'd spent a long time getting ready, and she wasn't going to chicken out now. Tonight, she wanted to feel feminine and pretty. Desirable.

She wanted to feel like a woman. For Dylan.

For herself.

AT NINE-FIFTEEN she heard the crunch of gravel on her driveway. She flew to the mirror, making sure her mascara hadn't smudged, and reapplied her lip gloss. Then she smoothed her hands down her dress again.

She should have worn something else. Dylan was

going to think she looked ridiculous, wearing this fancy dress for dinner at home.

Before she could dash into her bedroom and change, he knocked. Taking a deep breath, she walked into the living room and opened the door. He stood there holding two white cartons of Chinese food and a bottle of wine.

"Hi, Dylan." Her heart drummed against her chest. "Come on in."

"Charlotte." He walked inside and stopped abruptly. "Wow. You look…unbelievable."

"Thanks." She slid her hands behind her and rubbed her damp palms on her dress. "I probably should have changed, since we're not going anywhere, but…"

"No. I'm glad you didn't." His gaze traveled down to her legs, then back to her face. "Really glad."

"Come on into the kitchen," she said, yearning to reach for him but hesitant to make the first move. "We can open that bottle of wine and have dinner. What did you bring?"

"I don't remember."

"How can you not remember?" She turned and found him staring at her mouth.

"Remember what?" He dropped the cartons on the table and tangled his hand in her curls. "I'm not sure I remember my name," he said as he pulled her closer.

He brushed his mouth over hers, then nipped at her lower lip, and she realized she was trembling. "Dylan?"

"Oh, right, that's my name," he said, tucking her against him. "Are you hungry, Charlotte?" He trailed his mouth down her neck, then into the deep vee of her dress. "Do you want dinner?"

He nibbled at the swell of her breast above her bra, and she sucked in a breath. "No," she whispered.

"What do you want?" he murmured against her skin. His hand stroked her back, dipping to her hip and up again. His other hand held her bottom.

"You," she murmured, pressing her mouth against his. "I want you, Dylan."

"What are you going to do with me?"

"Maybe I'll start where we left off the other day," she said against his lips, his obvious desire for her giving her confidence. "Does that work for you?"

He groaned and she smiled. "I'll take that as a yes."

Her hands shook as she reached for his shirt and fumbled with the buttons. He stood still, only his mouth moving on hers. She finally got the last button undone and pushed the shirt off his shoulders.

"You're beautiful," she whispered. He was lean and hard, his abdomen ridged with muscle, his arms ropy and smooth. He shook the shirt onto the floor.

"It's my turn," he said, his voice thick. He tugged the zipper of her dress halfway down her back, but she squirmed away.

"I'm not finished," she said. She pushed the medal he wore to one side and the coarse hair tickled her palm. When she pressed her mouth to his chest, his fresh scent filled her senses as she tasted his skin, salty and musky and male. She swirled her tongue against the hard nub of his nipple and he shuddered.

"You're done, Charlotte," he said. "You are so done."

He reached behind her and unzipped her dress, then he pushed it off her shoulders and eased it over her hips. His eyes smoldered as he took in her lacy red bra and matching thong. "Are you trying to kill me?" he said, measuring the weight of her breasts in his hands. "Because it's working." He tugged at one nipple with his teeth, gently, but she could feel the heat of his mouth through the bra. Electricity flashed to her groin and she moved against him.

She reached for the waistband of his khaki slacks and shoved the button open. But when she began to lower the zipper, he grabbed her hands and kissed them.

"No," he said, his voice ragged. "Not yet." He pressed his mouth against her palm. "Bedroom."

"Around the corner," she gasped.

CHAPTER SIXTEEN

DYLAN CROWDED HER against the wall and devoured her mouth. Then he walked her backward into the bedroom. When they reached the bed, he lifted her onto the quilt and stood, looking at her. His gaze smoldered as it moved from her new bra to the nearly transparent thong that didn't hide a thing.

This wasn't Charlotte Burns, she thought dimly, sprawled on a bed in sexy underwear, watching a man look at her. This was a stranger. A woman who wasn't afraid to take what she wanted. Rising to one elbow, she unhooked her bra and let it slide down her arms. Dylan's eyes got even darker. Then he was on the bed beside her.

"Charlotte." He kissed her like he would die if he didn't. "You're destroying me."

He smoothed his hand over her breasts then lifted them, caressing their heavy weight. He brushed his fingers in a circle, teasing her, making her ache.

"For God's sake, Dylan," she groaned. "Touch me."

He smiled against her mouth. "Like this?"

He touched the tip of her nipple with one finger and she felt it contract into a tight nub. "Yes," she breathed.

"Or maybe like this?" Taking his mouth away from hers, he swirled his tongue around her, finally sucking the hard bud gently into his mouth.

She moved against him, her body's response shocking her. Maybe that afternoon on the couch wasn't a fluke. Maybe it really *was* different with Dylan.

Anticipation pouring through her, she reached for the button on his slacks. She needed to feel his skin against her, the hard length of his body against the softness of hers. Fumbling at his waist, she tried to unzip him.

He eased away from her. Quickly he pulled off his slacks and his boxers, retrieving a flat packet from his pocket before he let his pants drop to the floor.

She took the packet and tore it open before she could chicken out. She'd never performed such an intimate task before. Inching the condom down his hard, hot length, she pulled him close.

He kissed her again, his mouth seducing hers. She melted into him.

He caressed her hip, then she felt the scrap of thong being eased down her legs. His hand dipped between her legs, touching her, and she arched off the bed. "Dylan!"

"You're so sexy, Charlotte." He slid one finger over her, lingered. "So responsive." His finger moved in a circular motion. "You're making me crazy."

Her orgasm grabbed her without warning and she cried out, her hips rising off the bed. Then he was kissing her and sliding into her, and she shuddered against him.

He began to move, and her tension gathered again. As he moved faster, harder, she moved with him, and when he climaxed, she came along with him a second time.

DYLAN COULDN'T MOVE. Didn't want to move. Charlotte's legs were tangled with his and her head rested on his chest. She still held him tightly, as if she couldn't bear to be separated from him.

He never wanted to let her go. The realization alarmed him.

But he'd worry about that tomorrow. Tonight he wanted to stay with Charlotte, listen to her breathe as she slept and see her when she woke up. Her hair would be tousled and curly and her eyes would be slumberous and welcoming. He'd kiss her and they'd make love again. Then they'd shower together and he'd touch every inch of her gorgeous body as he washed her.

"Dylan?" Her voice was muffled against his chest, but he could tell she was smiling. She reached between them and ran her hand along the hard length of his erection. "Already?"

"The first time was just a practice run," he said, smiling down at her. "This time I'll get it right."

AT 2:00 A.M. HE SAT UP in Charlotte's bed. "I have to go," he said reluctantly. "I need to be there when Hayley gets up in the morning."

"I know," Charlotte answered. She sat up beside him and tucked the sheet beneath her arms.

He grinned as he tweaked the sheet. "Shy, Charlotte? Funny, you weren't acting very shy a while ago."

In the dim light he saw her blush and she dropped the sheet. "I'm a little nervous about this."

"Is that what you were?" he asked, bending to kiss her. "I thought you were sexy. Beautiful. Incredibly arousing."

"I mean this." She gestured at the bed. "The morning-after stuff. Even if it's still the middle of the night. I don't know what to say."

Her honesty made him want to get back into bed and kiss her senseless. "You can say, 'Dylan, you were incredible.' Or how about, 'You're the best ever.' Or my favorite, 'Let's do this again.'"

"How about all of the above?" she said, kneeling on the bed to kiss him back. "I wish you didn't have to go."

"So do I." He moved his mouth over hers and she laid her hand against his heart.

As he moved away, her hand tangled in the chain around his neck. "What's this?" she asked as she edged closer for a better look.

"It's a St. Andrew the Apostle medal." He glanced down at the oval medal of a saint holding a cross, the figure worn almost smooth after so many years.

Charlotte went absolutely still. She turned it over and studied the fish on the other side, then let it drop against his chest. "I didn't take you for a jewelry kind of guy, Dylan," she said lightly. But her hand shook as she eased away from him.

"It was my mother's," he said. "My father gave it to her before she left the orchard that summer. St. Andrew is the patron saint of unmarried women." He ran his finger over the medal's familiar surface. "It's the only thing I have that connects my parents."

Charlotte seemed pale in the muted light of her room. "I'm a selfish idiot," he said, standing. "I've kept you awake all night. You probably have to get up in a couple of hours."

"No, it's okay," she said, still staring at his chest. Finally she looked up at him, and her eyes were enormous.

"Hold that expression," he said. "As if you can't believe what just happened. I like knowing I put that look on your face." He shrugged into his shirt. "I can't wait to do it again."

She scrambled off the bed and reached for a skimpy silk robe, tugging hard on the belt. "Dylan…"

"Don't worry," he said. "I won't let Hayley sabotage us again. I'll take you out for that dinner we missed." He pulled her against him. "Wear that dress again, okay?"

He buttoned his pants and stuffed his socks into his pockets. Then he stepped into his shoes and headed for the door. The Chinese food he'd brought for dinner sat unopened on the kitchen table.

"Get some sleep, sweetheart," he said, kissing her a last time. "Keep up your strength. For tonight."

Before he could be tempted to stay longer, he slipped out the door.

Dylan's taillights grew smaller and the growl of his engine became fainter as his car sped away. Charlotte waited until she could no longer see it, then she closed the door.

My God.

She slid down the door until she was sitting on the floor, her head ready to burst.

The St. Andrew the Apostle medal had belonged to his mother.

Struggling to her feet, she went into the bedroom and opened her small jewelry box. A twin of Dylan's medal sat in a place of honor. It had been a gift from Gus the summer she became his first mate—St. Andrew was also the patron saint of fishermen.

Gus had ordered the medals from Scotland and given them to the people he loved. Kat had worn hers on a chain around her neck for a long time— maybe still did. Charlotte had worn hers until the day it tangled in fishline.

And Dylan's father had given one to Dylan's mother.

It was beyond belief that two different men working at the Van Allen orchard had given identical St. Andrew the Apostle medals.

The conclusion was inescapable—Gus was Dylan's father.

He had to be. Anything else was too coincidental, too far-fetched, to be believed.

So many things made sense now. The faint familiarity she'd seen in Dylan the first time she met him. Frances's discomfort with any talk about the orchard—she must have known that Gus had an affair the summer he'd worked there. Even Gus's reticence about the orchard. In all the years she'd known him, he'd never mentioned working there. Even though he'd known she was related to the Van Allens.

What should she do? Her head spinning, she sank onto the bed. Should she tell Gus? Dylan?

Neither of them?

How could she not tell Dylan? He was her lover, a man she was falling in love with. She knew how much he wanted to find his father. How important it was to him. How could she not tell him what he needed so badly to know?

"Frances," she murmured, remembering the woman's anguish as she'd talked about the problems she and Gus had that summer. How much more painful would it be if Frances found out that Gus had a son as a result of his infidelity?

She stifled a sob. Less than twenty-four hours ago, she'd promised Frances that Dylan's search for his father had nothing to do with her. Or Gus. That his search wouldn't hurt either of them.

If she told Gus that Dylan was his son, she'd break her promise to Frances.

And what about Kat? Her friend had always wanted a sibling. Now she had a brother. Didn't she have the right to know?

It was too much to process. Charlotte walked into

the kitchen and put the kettle on the stove. She needed tea. Frances's solution to any stressful situation.

Charlotte stood at the stove, waiting for the water to boil. Tears slid down her cheeks and sizzled as they hit the hot surface. She pictured Frances's hurt, Kat's bewilderment, Gus's...

Gus's what? How would he feel? Would he welcome a son? Would he resent being reminded of that painful time? She had no idea, but it was clear he wanted to forget all about the summer he'd worked at the orchard.

When the kettle whistled, she poured water over the tea bag, then sat at the kitchen table, her hands around the hot mug, staring out the window into the darkness. She wished with all her heart she hadn't seen that medal. That she still thought Stuart Van Allen was Dylan's father.

That she didn't have to choose who she'd hurt.

STEVE FILLETED the salmon from the morning charter as Charlotte talked to the two couples. Her face felt as if it would crack if she had to smile again. Finally, when the satisfied customers were gone, she slumped onto the bench in front of the office.

"Are you okay, Charlotte?" Steve hovered over her, worried. "You don't look right."

Of course she didn't look right. She'd been up all night. "I'm fine, Steve." She forced another smile. "Just tired. But thanks for asking."

"Maybe it's for the best our afternoon charter

canceled," he said as he tossed the fish scraps to the hovering gulls. Fish bones and scales splashed into the water as he sprayed the table. "You going home?"

"Yeah." She dragged herself off the bench. "Can you take care of the cleanup? You can add another hour to your time card."

"No problem. But you don't have to pay me extra," Steve said. He glanced over his shoulder. "For God's sake, Charlotte. You're letting me stay on your boat. I don't mind cleaning it."

"That wasn't part of the deal. But thanks, Steve. I appreciate it."

She headed toward her truck. A headache jackhammered at her temples and her eyes felt gritty and swollen. She'd get something to eat, she decided. She'd been too upset to eat that morning. And she'd missed dinner last night.

The memory of the night before, the reason she'd missed dinner, flashed through her like heat lightning. "Stop it," she muttered. She couldn't think about another night with Dylan until she figured out what she would say to him. *If* she would say anything to him.

"If you're talking to yourself, I hope it's about me."

She jumped at the sound of Dylan's voice and he eased away from the side of the marina, where he'd been lounging. "I thought you might be finishing your charter about now."

He swept her into his arms and kissed her. When she felt herself softening, pressing closer to him, she pulled away. "Where's Hayley?" she asked.

"She's playing soccer with Shelby and Elena. So I'm free for the next couple of hours." He grabbed her hand and pulled her toward his car. "I don't have much vacation left, so I want to see you as much as possible while I'm still here. I made some plans."

"What kind of plans?" She held back, frantically trying to think of an excuse to avoid going with him.

"It's a surprise," he said, swinging their joined hands.

"Dylan, I can't." She grabbed his arm to stop him. "I need to eat. And I need to sleep. That's all I'm capable of right now."

He stroked her arm and her skin tingled beneath his fingers. "Trust me, Charlotte. My surprise doesn't include jumping your bones." He kissed her again, his mouth lingering on hers. "Although I wouldn't say no if you asked."

"I can't," she said against his lips. But she twined her arms around his neck.

"Yeah, I know, you have another charter scheduled for this afternoon." He let her go, and guilt gnawed at her for not correcting him. "But you have a couple of hours. So come on."

He took her by the hand again and led her to his car. As they drove away, she asked where they were going. He just smiled. Ten minutes later, they pulled into the parking lot of the Sturgeon Falls Canal Recreation Area.

"I brought a picnic," Dylan said as he got out. "I suspect you don't have enough picnics, Charlotte. We need to address that deficit."

"A picnic?" She stepped out of the car and looked at the nearly deserted expanse of sand in front of her. Seagulls wandered along the water's edge, dancing sideways as waves lapped at their feet. Dunes covered with tough sea grass rose behind the beach. "How did you find out about this park? No one but locals come here."

He gave her a smug smile. "It just so happens that I know a few locals."

Charlotte's heart squeezed in her chest. "You went to a lot of trouble for me."

"Why wouldn't I?" He stopped in the middle of the path. The seed plumes of the grasses next to the trail swayed when he dropped the picnic basket. "You're worth a lot of trouble." He held her face and kissed her again. "Besides, I was hoping I could cop a feel behind the dunes."

Don't make me laugh. Don't remind me how much I enjoy your company. Don't make this more difficult than it already is.

"Are you sure about that?" she asked, forcing a lightness into her voice she didn't feel. "In the sand? That sounds painful."

He wiggled his eyebrows as he picked up the basket again. "My creativity will awe and amaze you, sweetheart."

Her heart squeezed again at the endearment. "I can't wait."

Two hours later, when Dylan dropped her off at the marina, she watched him drive away with a lump in her throat. He'd been a perfect companion, feeding her a gourmet lunch beneath a huge umbrella, then sitting beside her as she drifted to sleep. And when he'd woken her with a kiss, he'd managed to brush his fingers across her breast.

She opened her truck door to a blast of ovenlike heat and sank onto the scorching upholstery. What should she do? Who should she tell?

Daylight and lunch with Dylan hadn't revealed any answers. It had just made her dilemma more difficult.

CHAPTER SEVENTEEN

TWO MORNINGS LATER, exhausted and numb, Charlotte waved goodbye with a fixed smile as her customers drove away.

"See you back here at two o'clock?" Steve asked over his shoulder.

"Two is good," she said, heading toward the boat.

"I'll clean up," Steve called, and she nodded without turning. She'd get her purse and go home. Maybe she'd be able to sleep.

She'd tossed and turned the night before, getting very little sleep after telling Dylan she couldn't see him that evening. Their conversation had run through her head on an endless loop, with Dylan asking if something was wrong and her denying it. After an increasingly stilted conversation and several uncomfortable silences, she'd quietly said goodbye and hung up.

There was no way to fix what was wrong between them without telling Dylan the truth about Gus. And she wanted desperately to fix it. She wanted to see Dylan again, to kiss him, to watch him laugh.

She had no idea how to bridge the gulf looming between them.

Where did her loyalties lie? With Dylan? With Gus and Frances? Did she even have the right to make a decision? Should she just tell both Dylan and Gus and let them work it out themselves?

Her footsteps slowed as she neared Gus's boat. She'd spent so many hours here with him. They'd forged a bond that was as close as any father and daughter. When he found out he had a son, would that change?

Ashamed of herself for doubting Gus, for letting her fears stop her from doing the right thing, she stopped at the boat. His door was open. Making an abrupt decision, she called, "Hey, Gus."

He didn't answer. He was probably down in the galley. Jumping onto the deck and feeling the boat rock beneath her feet, she stuck her head inside.

Gus lay on the floor, his eyes closed. Unmoving.

"Gus!" She dropped to her knees beside him before she noticed the dark stain on the brown rug. It was wet and sticky. When she touched it, her fingers came away red.

Her hand shook as she struggled to pull her phone out of her pocket and dial 911. Finally a woman said, "Nine-one-one center. How can I help you?"

"I need an ambulance. Right away. Gus Macauley is hurt. He's unconscious and his head is bleeding."

"What is your location, please?"

"The marina, Sturgeon Falls Marina."

There was a pause. "All right, ma'am, an ambulance is on its way." Her voice was detached and soothing. "Tell me exactly where you are."

"We're on his boat, the *Wild Hair*." She bent closer and laid her hand on Gus's chest, saying a prayer of thanksgiving when she felt a faint rise and fall. When she took her hand away, her bloody handprint remained on his blue chambray work shirt.

"Where is the boat, ma'am?"

"It's at the marina!" Charlotte murmured, "Gus. Wake up."

"You need to be more specific," the person on the other end interrupted.

"Right. Sorry. Third pier from the right. About halfway down on the left side."

"Thank you, ma'am. Is the victim breathing?"

He wasn't a *victim*. This was Gus. "Yes, I can feel his chest move."

"Can you see a wound on his head?"

She bent closer and saw a gaping wound on his scalp. His gray hair was matted with the blood still steadily dripping from the gash. "Yes." She swallowed.

"Don't move his head," the dispatcher said sharply. "The paramedics will be there momentarily."

Charlotte dropped the phone. Seeing Gus's flannel shirt on a chair, she grabbed it and held it against the wound. The sound of an approaching siren mixed with the dispatcher's voice, demanding that she come back to the phone. Long moments later, she heard the sound of feet running down the pier.

"Step aside, ma'am," said a stocky paramedic as he squatted next to Gus. "What happened here?"

"I don't know." She focused on Gus's head.

Wounds needed pressure. To stop the bleeding. "I found him like this."

Another paramedic listened to Gus's chest, looked at his pupils, then shoved his sleeve up past his elbow and took his blood pressure. The first paramedic gently removed her hand from behind Gus's head, then fastened a neck brace in place. After they started an IV, they slid a body board beneath Gus and loaded him onto a stretcher.

"I'm going with him in the ambulance," Charlotte said as she walked beside the stretcher. In the sunlight, Gus's face was paper white. Blood was smeared on the body board and the white sheet on the stretcher.

"Are you his daughter?"

"I'm like a daughter to him."

"Only family is supposed to ride in the ambulance. Sorry, miss," one of the paramedics answered.

"I *am* family, and I'm not leaving him," she said, taking Gus's hand. She was shocked at how cold it was.

The paramedics exchanged glances. One of them shrugged. "Fine. I'm not going to waste time arguing with you. He needs to get to the hospital."

Charlotte clung to Gus's hand as the ambulance raced through the streets. Once they reached the hospital, they rolled the stretcher into the emergency room. A nurse stepped in front of Charlotte as she tried to follow. "You'll have to wait out here."

"I'm staying with him," Charlotte retorted. She stared at the nurse until the older woman moved aside.

"You get in the way or get hysterical, I'll throw you out myself," the nurse warned.

"Don't worry. I won't." Charlotte brushed past the nurse and followed the stretcher holding Gus into a tiny cubicle. After a few minutes, another nurse stepped in. She looked at the wound on his head, did a quick assessment, then turned to Charlotte. "Did he fall?"

"I don't know," Charlotte answered. "He was unconscious when I found him."

The nurse's eyes were full of sympathy as she looked at Charlotte. "We have to do some tests on your father," she said. "We need you to sign the permission forms."

"He isn't my father," Charlotte said, her heart twisting. "His daughter is Kat Macauley. She's a doctor on staff here."

"This is Kat's dad?" the nurse said.

"Yes."

"Is she on her way?"

"I haven't called her yet. I'll sign the forms."

"Sorry, honey. It has to be family." She took Charlotte by the arm and pulled her gently out of the cubicle. "I'll call Kat. You probably have other people to call. Why don't you do that in the waiting room?"

"Kat would want me to stay with him," Charlotte said.

"We'll ask her," the nurse replied. She steered Charlotte toward the swinging doors. "You wait out here."

Before Charlotte could answer, she was on the other side of the doors. She pushed one of them open and was halfway through it when the nurse saw her. "Don't make me call security, honey." Her voice gentled. "We'll take good care of him."

She finally backed out. Squabbling about her right to stay with Gus wasn't going to get him treated any faster.

Pacing in the designated cell phone area, she called Frances. "This is Charlotte," she said, gripping the phone tightly. "Gus had an accident on the boat. He's at the hospital."

"Oh, my God. Is he all right?"

"He's unconscious." She remembered the pool of blood beneath his head. "It looks like he fell."

"Stay with him, Charlotte. I'll be right there."

Before Charlotte could answer, Frances had disconnected. Charlotte called Kat, but Kat's nurse told her that Kat had already left for the hospital. Then, taking a deep breath, she dialed again.

"Dylan, it's Charlotte."

"Hey, Charlotte," he said warily, and she bit her lip, regretting the painful pauses and omissions of their phone conversation the evening before.

She couldn't think about that. "I'm at the hospital," she said as she struggled to keep her voice steady. "It's Gus. He's hurt." She swallowed around the lump in her throat. "I found him on the floor of his boat. Bleeding."

"I'll be right there."

The phone clicked and Charlotte snapped her phone closed. She paced the waiting room, ignoring the other occupants, counting the minutes. Just as she had decided to go back to Gus and the hell with the rules, Dylan ran into the room.

"Charlotte," he said, wrapping his arms around

her. She collapsed against him, absorbing his warmth, grateful for his strength. She hadn't realized how cold she was.

"Dylan. I'm so glad you're here."

"Sweetheart," Dylan said, taking her face in his hands. "I'm glad you called. So I could be here for you."

Charlotte began to cry, her tears soaking Dylan's shirt. She felt like a fool, but Dylan stroked her head, murmuring, "Okay. It's going to be okay."

"He was unconscious," Charlotte choked out. "There was a cut on his head. So much blood."

"Head wounds bleed a lot." He smoothed down her hair. "That doesn't mean it was serious."

"There was stuff I didn't tell him," she said into Dylan's shoulder. "Important stuff." And now she might not have the chance. Gus might never know he had a son.

"He knows how much you love him."

She'd been so wrong to withhold the information from Gus. More tears spilled onto Dylan's shirt, and he pulled her into a corner. Away from the other people in the waiting room.

"Charlotte?" Frances asked from behind her, and Charlotte reluctantly let Dylan go.

"What happened?" The older woman grabbed Charlotte's hands. "Tell me everything."

"There isn't much to tell." She repeated the story, watching Frances's shock and fright. "They wouldn't let me wait with him."

"Kat's in there now. She picked me up on her way

to the hospital." Frances looked around, dazed. "She said it might be a while."

"You should both sit down." Dylan guided Frances to a chair, then eased Charlotte down next to her. "Hold on. I'll be right back."

He reappeared a few minutes later with two cups of coffee. It was too hot and too strong, and her stomach churned as she took a sip. But the foam cup warmed her hands. Frances muttered her thanks, then set it aside.

"Tea?" Dylan asked, nodding at Frances.

She agreed, and he walked back to the vending machine. When he set a cup of tea next to Frances, she looked startled. "Thank you, Mr. Smith."

"It's Dylan," he said, sitting next to Charlotte and taking her hand.

Frances nodded, but she looked at Charlotte. "Why hasn't Kat told us what's happening?"

"They probably don't know anything yet," Charlotte answered, trying to compose herself. She couldn't fall apart in front of Frances. She had to be strong for her. "They told me they had to do a bunch of tests."

"You and Kat and Mrs. Macauley probably want some family time," Dylan said to her quietly. "Do you want me to leave?"

"No." She reached for his hand. "You should stay." She couldn't meet his gaze. "You need to stay."

"Are you sure?"

"Please, Dylan. Stay. If you can. You need to be here for Gus."

"*You* need to be here for Gus. You're part of the family. I'm here for you." He squeezed her hand. "Let me call Kendall and see if she can watch Hayley."

A few moments later, he closed his phone and said, "Kendall can keep Hayley for as long as she needs to. If you're sure you want me here?"

"I'm sure." She wanted Dylan here for herself, as well as for Gus. And the realization flooded her with guilt all over again. "Where is Kat?" She headed toward the treatment area. "I need to know what's going on."

Dylan followed her and pulled her back into the chair. "Kat's a doctor," he said. "She knows the people here. She'll come out and tell us as soon as she knows anything."

"You're Mr. Calm, aren't you?" she said, her lip quivering.

"Someone has to be," he said. "And since I'm not a relative, I get to be the calm one."

Charlotte's eyes filled and she reached for him. *Not a relative.* What had she done?

CHAPTER EIGHTEEN

FINALLY, AFTER WHAT SEEMED to Dylan like hours, Kat came through the emergency room doors and dropped into the chair next to her mother. "They're doing a CT scan," she said. "They're afraid he has a skull fracture." She swallowed. "He has symptoms of swelling in his head. Affecting his brain."

"What does that mean?" Frances whispered.

"They don't know yet, Mom," Kat answered, but she didn't meet her mother's eyes. "He might need surgery."

Dylan took a deep breath. "Blood clot?" he asked.

She nodded, pressing her lips together.

"Brain surgery?" Charlotte asked. Her face got even whiter. "Oh, God."

He wanted to pull her into his arms, to comfort her. But she'd tried to put distance between them the last couple of days, and now Kat and Frances were sitting next to her. So instead he tucked a strand of hair behind her ear. "Gus is a tough old bird," he said. "He's going to be fine."

"You don't know that. Don't patronize me."

She took a deep breath. "I'm sorry," she whispered. "I'm sorry."

"It's okay." He put his arm around her. "I understand."

"You couldn't possibly understand," she said, her voice full of despair.

Her words stabbed into him like sharp knives. "No. I've never had a father to worry about," he said. "But I can imagine how it would feel."

"That's not what I meant," she said, clearly horrified. "Not what I meant at all."

She looked as if she wanted to say more, but Frances interrupted. "Katriona. I want the truth. Is your father going to die?"

Dylan saw the fear on Kat's face.

"I don't know, Mom," she said. "I hope not." She fingered her stethoscope. "They're doing everything they can. They'll come and talk to us after they read the CT scan."

"I told him to stay away from that boat until he was stronger," Frances whispered. "He must have lost his balance and fallen."

Kat's mouth tightened. "The boat didn't have anything to do with this. He was attacked. Someone hit him in the head. With a gun, they think."

"What?" Dylan turned to stare at Kat. "Someone attacked Gus?"

"Yes. That's what the E.R. doc said." Kat swallowed. "I looked at the wound, and I think she's right. I saw plenty of those kinds of injuries when I was doing my residency in Milwaukee."

"Who would want to hurt Gus?" Frances asked, and started crying again.

"Those developers," Dylan said, anger churning inside him. He looked at Frances. "Gus told me two guys came to your house the other day. Do you remember them?"

"Yes. Do you think they're the ones who attacked him?"

"I'd say there's a good chance. And if it wasn't them, I bet they're involved somehow. The police should know about this."

"We called the police after we realized what probably caused the wound," Kat said. "They're talking to the E.R. docs right now. They want to talk to Charlotte when they're finished."

"You should talk to them, as well, Mrs. Macauley," Dylan said. "Give them a description of the men who came to your house. The police might even want you to work with an artist to get a picture of them."

"How do you know so much about this?" Frances asked.

"I'm an investigative reporter. I figure things out." His smile was grim. "I spend lots of time with the cops."

When the police emerged from the treatment area a half hour later, he stood to the side and watched as they questioned Charlotte and then Frances.

Charlotte was confident, strong and decisive. The woman who'd sobbed against his chest earlier was gone. In her place was the Charlotte who didn't appear to need anything. Or anybody.

The Charlotte who'd pushed him out of her life after the most shattering, life-altering lovemaking he'd ever experienced.

If she thought she could get rid of him that easily, he was going to prove how wrong she was.

HAYLEY DIDN'T like hospitals.

Her Aunt Joan had been in the hospital a *lot,* and she'd had to go with her mom to visit her aunt. She didn't like the smell, and she didn't like hearing the sick people cry and moan. She wanted to stay at Van Allen House this morning and play soccer with Shelby.

But Shelby and her sister weren't going to be home, so she had to go with her dad, and he wanted to visit Gus. She snuck a glance at her father. He seemed sad. Was Gus going to die?

When they walked into the waiting room, Charlotte was sitting on the couch, with her head back and her eyes closed. Her hair was hanging out of her ponytail and her clothes were all wrinkled. She looked like a mess, Hayley thought. What would her dad think when he saw Charlotte?

"Hey," he said as he sat beside Charlotte. "How are you doing?"

Charlotte jerked awake. "Dylan." She looked like she was going to hug him, but then she saw Hayley. "Hayley. Thank you for coming." She smiled, but she seemed sad, too.

"Is Gus better?" Hayley asked, suddenly frightened. It wasn't good when the adults were sad.

Charlotte bit her lip. "We think so. He had

surgery last night, and that fixed what was wrong. We'll tell him you were here, after he wakes up. He'll be glad you came to see him."

Like she'd had a choice. But she shrugged. "Sure."

"Were you here all night?" her dad asked Charlotte.

Charlotte nodded, removing the band holding her ragged ponytail and pulling the strands together before replacing it. "Kat had to get back to Regan, and Frances was completely exhausted. I told them I'd stay the night and leave when they got here in the morning."

Her dad sat next to Charlotte, talking to her, and Hayley looked at a magazine. After a while, two women walked into the waiting room, and Hayley recognized them from the fish boil. Regan's mom, Kat, and Mrs. Macauley. Charlotte and her dad stood up and started talking to them.

She should have brought a book. She always brought a book when she went to the hospital with her mom. She heard beeping, and she wandered through the door. There were a bunch of windows lining a hall. Then she stopped. That was Gus in a bed by one of those windows.

He had a white bandage around his head, and a tube hooked up to his arm. And he was lying so still! Like he was dead. She stared at him, willing him to move.

"You shouldn't be in here, Hayley," Charlotte said from behind her. Charlotte put her hands on her shoulders. "Gus is sleeping. That's why he's not moving."

"Are you sure?" Her voice sounded like it

belonged to someone else. A baby's voice. "Are you sure he's not dead?"

"Positive," Charlotte said firmly. "If you watch carefully, you can see him breathing." She squatted next to her. "See? Watch the blankets move."

Hayley stared at Gus. "There! He breathed!"

"Right." Charlotte stood and turned her away from the window. "Come on back into the waiting room, okay?"

Hayley heard beeping from some of the other rooms, and she smelled that hospital smell. "I don't like it here," she said. She wished she didn't sound like a baby.

Charlotte squeezed her shoulder. "I don't, either," she said. "I hate seeing Gus in the hospital."

"My dad said Gus is like your dad."

"He is." Charlotte let go of her, and Hayley wished she hadn't. It felt kind of good to have Charlotte holding on to her. "I love Gus very much, and I'm scared," Charlotte said. "It's okay if you are, too."

"Only babies are scared of stuff."

Charlotte smiled, but it was a sad kind of smile. "There are lots of things adults are scared of, too, Hayley. Sometimes they just pretend better than kids."

"Yeah?"

"Yeah." Charlotte reached out as if to touch her hair, then dropped her hand. "How about a soda?"

"No, thanks."

"Do you want something to eat?" Charlotte fiddled with her earring, and Hayley remembered her promise from the day of the boat trip.

"Could we maybe go get my ears pierced?" she asked impulsively.

Charlotte looked surprised. "Right now?"

"Yeah." Hayley rubbed her hands on her shorts. "Gus is sleeping, right? So he won't know that we're gone. It would only take a little while." And it would get her out of this hospital.

"I'm not sure what your dad has planned," Charlotte said. "He might have other things to do."

"I'll ask him."

Her dad was talking to Kat, and Hayley poked him in the back. "Dad, is it okay if Charlotte takes me to get my ears pierced?"

"This is hardly the time," he said. He shot Charlotte a puzzled look. "I think Charlotte is going home."

"I don't mind," Charlotte said, standing next to her. "It'll be fun."

Her dad looked at Charlotte for a long time. "You need to get some sleep," he finally said. His voice sounded all lovey-dovey. But Hayley didn't mind too much. Charlotte was going to take her to get her ears pierced. Maybe she wasn't that bad.

"I got some sleep last night," Charlotte answered. "I'm fine." She nudged Hayley. "We could both use some girl time. Right, Hayley?"

"Right. Girl time." Whatever that meant.

"All right. Your mom said it was okay. Behave yourself for Charlotte," her dad said to her.

Hayley rolled her eyes. Like she would do something stupid when *she'd* asked Charlotte to get her out of here. "I will."

"Ready to go?" Charlotte asked. She smiled at Hayley's dad, but her eyes were sad.

"Are you sure it's okay?" Hayley asked, worried.

"Absolutely."

Charlotte needed to get out of the hospital. Away from Dylan. Every time she looked at him, a crushing weight settled on her chest. And she was too tired to deal with it right now.

"Maybe we shouldn't do this," Hayley said in a small voice.

Charlotte looked down at her worried face and pushed thoughts of Dylan away. "This was a great idea, Hayley. I'm glad you thought of it."

"Are you sure?"

"I'm positive."

Apparently, Hayley's desperation to leave was stronger than her aversion to Charlotte. Maybe Hayley would revert to her old, hostile self once Gus was out of the hospital and things were back to normal.

It didn't matter. They both needed out.

"What kind of earrings do you want to get?" Charlotte asked Hayley as they climbed into her truck.

"I don't know." The girl looked at the dangly silver earrings Charlotte wore. "I like those."

"Really?" Charlotte fingered hers, surprised Hayley would admit it. "We'll see if we can find some like this for later. But first you need a pair of post earrings. You have to wear them for a long time before you can take them out and wear something else. They have stones in lots of different colors to choose from."

"Maybe I'll get blue. My soccer uniform is blue."

"I like blue," Charlotte said, angling her truck into a parking spot on the street near the jewelry store. "Let's go see what they have."

An hour later they were back in the hospital parking lot. Hayley touched the blue earrings, then pulled down the visor and looked in the mirror. "These are so cool."

"They are." Charlotte grinned. "And you handled it like a pro. Not like that boy who squealed before they even touched him."

Hayley laughed. "Yeah, he was a real dork."

"You were strong, Hayley. I'm proud of you."

"Thanks, Charlotte." She smoothed her hands over her shorts. "Thanks for taking me to get my ears pierced," she said in a low voice. "I was pretty snotty to you."

"Don't worry about it. You apologized and it's forgotten."

Hayley played with the bag in her lap that held two more pairs of earrings. "I guess I don't mind if you're going out with my dad. You're pretty cool."

Charlotte stared out the window. "Thanks. That means a lot to me," she said, trying to keep her voice steady. Would Dylan still be interested after he learned the truth? "But your dad is about finished with his story so he's going back to Green Bay. We might not be going out much longer."

"Really? I thought you liked my dad."

Oh, God, how to handle this? "I do," she said. "But I live here in Sturgeon Falls. It's easier to go out with someone if you live close by."

"Oh." Her face brightened. "Maybe we'll see you when we come to visit Gus. Dad said we could come back and fish with Gus when he's better."

"Gus will love that," Charlotte said. She hoped Hayley couldn't sense her pain. "Maybe I'll see you then." She opened her car door. "Ready to go back upstairs?"

"I guess." But Hayley made no effort to get out.

"You don't like being here, do you?" Charlotte asked.

Hayley shook her head. "It reminds me of my Aunt Joan," she said quietly. "Mom cries when we visit my aunt."

Another minefield. "It can be sad when people are sick. We're all worried about Gus, but the doctors said he's going to be fine. Once he wakes up, you can talk to him about fishing."

"He has that bandage on his head. And all those tubes," she said. Her lip quivered.

"It's scary for me to see him like that, too." Taking a chance, she reached for Hayley, and the girl clung to her. "But he's going to wake up real soon, and then he'll just be Gus again." She smiled. "He'll probably complain about the tubes and the bandage."

"You think so?"

"I know so," Charlotte said, hopping out of the truck. "I've known Gus a lot longer than you have, and trust me, he's going to be crabby."

As they walked toward the hospital, Hayley slipped her hand into Charlotte's. Startled, Charlotte looked down at her, but Hayley acted like it was the most natural thing in the world.

"I don't think Gus is crabby," Hayley said.

Charlotte laughed. "You wait until you've spent a little time around him. Then you'll see crabby. But you know what works with Gus? Teasing him. He loves it when you sass him back when he's grouchy."

"Really?"

"Yep. Gus is a sucker for mouthy girls."

"Were you a mouthy girl?"

"I took first prize in sass," she said, grinning down at Hayley. "You ask Gus about it sometime."

"Really?"

"Yeah. But don't tell him I told you to do it, okay?"

"Okay."

Hayley nodded happily, and regret washed over Charlotte. Hayley was a bright, interesting girl. Charlotte hoped she had a chance to get to know her better.

"How about we go upstairs and see how Gus is doing? Your dad is probably feeling sad about Gus, too," Charlotte said. "I think he feels better when you're with him."

"Yeah?" Hayley stood straighter. "Then I guess we should hurry."

As they walked through the E.R. waiting room toward the ICU waiting room, Charlotte saw Steve Jacobs and his mom, huddled in chairs. Steve had his arm around his mom, and she was resting her head on his shoulder. Dread filled Charlotte as she watched them. She was afraid she knew why they were at the emergency room. Charlotte steered Hayley away from them.

When they reached the intensive care waiting room, Hayley rushed over to Dylan to show off her newly pierced ears. "I was very brave," she said proudly. "Even Charlotte said so."

"Is that right?" Dylan smiled at Charlotte. "I hope you thanked her for taking you to have holes put in your ears."

"Da-a-ad," Hayley said, rolling her eyes. "Of course I thanked her."

Frances was in one of the chairs but Kat was gone. Charlotte crouched in front of Frances. "I have something to do for a few minutes," she said. "I'll be right back."

"I'll stay with her until you get back," Dylan said in a low voice.

"Thank you. I won't be long."

CHAPTER NINETEEN

CHARLOTTE HURRIED into the E.R. waiting room, then hesitated. Maybe she shouldn't have come down here. Maybe she was intruding. She rubbed her forehead. Maybe she was too tired to think straight.

Before she could leave, Steve looked up and saw her. Instead of embarrassment, she saw anger and resolve on his face. Charlotte walked over to him.

"Steve. Mrs. Jacobs. Is everything okay?"

"My mom is hurt," Steve growled.

"I'm sorry, Mrs. Jacobs," Charlotte said gently. "Is there anything I can do?"

"Thank you, Charlotte, but no. I'm fine." Helen Jacobs kept her face hidden.

"She is not fine," Steve said. His arm tightened around his mother and he clenched his jaw. "My father hit her again. I think he broke her arm."

"Shh," Mrs. Jacobs warned. "Not so loud."

"I've kept quiet for too long," Steve said. He sounded different. Like he'd grown up overnight. "Maybe everyone *should* know what he does to you."

"Not here, Steve," Mrs. Jacobs whispered. "Please."

Helen lifted her head to look at him. The right side of her face had a fresh bruise. Her eye was bright red, and the skin around it was swollen and purple.

"You're not going back there," Steve said. "I won't let you."

Charlotte didn't want to add to the woman's humiliation, but she wanted to help. "You could take her to my house," she murmured to Steve. "I'll stay on the boat." Maybe it would be easier to figure out what to do if she didn't have to face reminders of Dylan and their lovemaking every time she walked in her front door. She cleared her throat. "I didn't get a chance to call you, but I won't be taking out any charters for the next few days."

Steve looked puzzled, and she swallowed hard as she added, "Gus was hurt. He's in intensive care."

"What happened?"

"Long story. He had surgery last night, but he should be fine." She peered around him. "Mrs. Jacobs, if you'd like to stay in my house for a few days, you're more than welcome. I need to stay on my boat."

Shame colored Mrs. Jacobs's unbruised cheek. "Thank you, Charlotte, but that's not necessary."

"It's up to you," Charlotte said, trying to keep her voice light. "But it's there if you need it."

Before the woman could answer, Charlotte stood up. "You're more than welcome to stay at my house," she said to Steve. "There's a key under the biggest flowerpot on the back porch." She touched his shoulder and moved away. "I need to get back to Gus."

"Thanks, Charlotte."

"You're welcome." When she got back to the intensive care waiting room, Dylan was talking to Sheriff Godfrey. Hayley was slumped in a chair, reading a magazine. There was no sign of Kat or Frances.

Dylan reached for her hand. "Kat and Frances are in with Gus. The sheriff is here to talk to Frances, but I thought I'd tell him what I know, as long as I'm here."

"Good. The more information, the better." She let him go as Dylan turned his attention to the sheriff. He continued his detailed description of the kids he'd helped chase from Gus's boat, and the men on Charlotte's charter who'd acted so odd.

"You willing to work with an artist?" the sheriff asked.

"Absolutely. The sooner the better."

The sheriff nodded. "I'll try to get Mrs. Macauley together with an artist today or tomorrow. We'll do all the pictures at the same time."

"Fine. Just let me know where and when."

"Will do."

Dylan turned to her. "Annie called. She's on her way to pick Hayley up. I have to go, but I'll be back later." He bent and brushed his mouth over hers, then stood up.

Hayley smiled tentatively. "Thanks again for taking me to get my ears pierced."

"You're welcome, Hayley. I'll see you soon." She hoped. She watched Dylan and Hayley walk down the hall.

After telling the sheriff what had happened on her

charter and describing the men, she waited until he'd finished writing and closed his notebook.

"You're going to give this case your full attention, aren't you, Sheriff?"

"Of course. I give all my cases my full attention," he said warily. "I was elected to protect all the citizens of Door County."

"I'm glad to hear that, Sheriff Godfrey. Steve Jacobs is downstairs in the E.R. waiting room with his mother, and she needs your protection. She's hurt." Charlotte dug her fingers into her thighs. "I think her husband hit her."

"Did she tell you that?" The sheriff spoke too quickly.

"She hardly spoke to me at all. But I think you need to talk to her."

"Stay away from the Jacobs family," he said ominously. "You have no business interfering in their affairs."

She raised her eyebrows, annoyance washing away her exhaustion. "That's an odd thing to say. Has one of them complained that I'm harassing them?"

His face got red. "That's immaterial."

"I don't think it is. Have you received a complaint about me?"

He stared at her, bristling, but she didn't look away. Finally he muttered, "No. I haven't received any complaints."

"So why would you tell me to stay away from them?"

"The Jacobs family is going through hard times," he answered. But he wouldn't meet her gaze.

"I know they are, Sheriff Godfrey. A lot of other people know it, too. And we all know what those hard times are. You just said it's your job to protect the citizens of this county. Did you mean everyone except women with powerful husbands?"

"I haven't gotten any calls from the Jacobses."

"No?" She was angry now. "I know for a fact Steve has called you and told you exactly what his father is doing to his mother."

The sheriff's face got redder. "Steve is just a kid."

"Steve is twenty-two years old. He's a man trying to protect his mother. You should be ashamed of yourself."

"Things are complicated, Charlotte. You don't understand."

"I think I understand too well. Lyle Jacobs controls a lot of jobs in this county. And if you go against him, you're afraid he'll make sure you don't get reelected." She narrowed her eyes. "I have news for you, Sheriff. If you don't do anything about Lyle Jacobs beating his wife, *I'll* make sure you don't get reelected. I'll make sure everyone knows how you're ignoring a woman who is being beaten. I'll make sure they know your job is more important to you than justice."

"Big talk, Charlotte." He sneered.

"You think it's talk?" she asked. "Gus and Frances and Kat and I know a lot of people in Sturgeon Falls. It's not going to take much to make sure everyone knows what's going on in the Jacobses' house. And how you're ignoring it."

"Fine. When Helen Jacobs calls me to complain that her husband is hitting her, I'll take care of it."

"You're not going to wait until she calls, because Mrs. Jacobs isn't going to call you. She's too afraid of her husband. She's downstairs in the E.R. waiting room right now. She's got bruises on her face and a possible broken arm. I expect you to arrest her husband."

Panic flickered across his face. "I won't do that without a complaint."

"You've got one. From me. Now go talk to them. Steve will tell you exactly what he's seen his father do."

The sheriff rubbed his hand across his face. "You're a pain in the ass, Charlotte. You know that?"

"You have no idea how much of a pain in the ass I can be. Now get a backbone and go to the E.R. You have a crime victim down there and you need to take her statement."

He pushed himself out of the chair and walked out the door without looking back. She watched him disappear, then slumped in her chair.

"Well done, Charlotte," Kat said from the door.

Charlotte spun around. "I didn't see you."

"I didn't want to interrupt." Kat dropped into the chair next to her. "It's about time someone put the fear of God into the sheriff."

"I probably just antagonized him, but I'm too tired to care. How's Gus?" she asked.

"Still unconscious, but they're cutting back on the

sedative. He should be waking up by this evening. I'm going to take Mom home and make her rest until after dinner. You'd better go home, too. You look like hell."

"I feel like hell." That's what guilt did to you. "I'll head home in a while."

"Good. Dad is going to need us all once he's awake," Kat said. Exhaustion had made her face gray. "We have to take care of ourselves. For him."

"I know." Her eyes were dry and her head pounded with exhaustion. "I want to see him again before I go. I'll stay until the next time they'll let me into his room."

Kat stood up. "Let me talk to the nurse."

A few minutes later, Kat beckoned to Charlotte. "She says you can see him now."

Charlotte stepped into Gus's cubicle and pulled a chair up next to his bed. The heart monitor beeped softly in the background, and lights flashed on the IV stand. His hand was cold and dry, and she wrapped her fingers around it, as much to reassure herself as to warm him up.

"Gus, I'm so sorry," she whispered. "There's something I should have told you. Something important. And now I'm afraid I'll never get that chance. I'm not sure you can hear me, but I have to tell you. In case…"

She swallowed hard. Gus was *not* going to die. He couldn't die. Not without learning the truth.

"It's about Dylan. Hayley's father. He's…" She bit her lip. "He's your son, Gus. He has the medal you gave his mother. Hayley is your granddaughter."

She thought Gus's hand moved between hers, just a twitch. "I promise I'll tell you as soon as you're awake. I was so wrong to keep this from you." And from Dylan. She needed to tell him, too. As soon as possible.

"What are you talking about, Charlotte?" Frances said from the doorway where she and Kat stood.

Charlotte dropped Gus's hand and shifted in the chair. Frances's face was white and her mouth trembled. "What are you doing here? I thought you were going home."

"I forgot my handbag," Frances said, nodding at the purse on the floor. She stepped closer. "Did I hear you say that Dylan Smith is Gus's son?"

Oh, no. What had she done? She looked from Frances's stricken expression to Kat's shocked one. "I'm sorry, Frances. Kat. So sorry. I didn't mean for you to find out like this." She jumped to her feet. "I shouldn't have said anything. I wouldn't have, if I'd known you were there. But I feel so guilty for not telling Gus sooner. Before he was attacked. And now I'm afraid…"

"He's not going to die." Frances looked at Gus with a mixture of love and sorrow. "He's too ornery." She took Charlotte by the arm and tugged her toward the door. "We can't discuss this in here."

The lights in the waiting room were too bright. Charlotte wanted to close her eyes, to block everything out—the wrong decision she'd made, the memory of Gus lying so still, the hurt on Frances's face.

"Why do you think Dylan is Gus's son?" Frances asked.

Kat put her arm around her mother's shoulders. "What's going on, Charlotte?"

Charlotte stared at the two women in front of her, the women she was closest to. Her family. How was she supposed to tell Frances about her husband's infidelity? How could she tell Kat that her father had had an affair while married to her mother? "I'm sorry," she whispered.

"I already knew about that woman at the orchard," Frances said. "Gus told me about her a long time ago."

"What woman at the orchard?" Kat asked.

Frances patted Kat's arm. "I'll tell you later." She looked at Charlotte. "I'm assuming your reporter is that woman's son."

"Yes." Charlotte pulled out the medal Gus had given her. She'd kept it in her pocket since seeing Dylan's. "Dylan has a medal like this. Identical to this. I saw it the other night when…" She felt her face redden. "It doesn't matter when I saw it. Dylan has one. His mother got it from his father when they both worked at the Van Allen orchard."

"Dad never worked at the orchard," Kat said. She looked from Charlotte to her mother. "Did he?"

"Later, Kat. You can't tell Gus, Charlotte. Promise me."

"I can't promise you that," Charlotte answered, shocked. "Gus has a right to know. And so does Dylan."

"I know that. Just don't tell him yet. Not until Gus is stronger. Not until he can deal with it."

"I think Gus can deal with a lot. I'm not sure we need to protect him."

"Just until he's himself again."

"That's not fair to Dylan," Charlotte said.

"I don't care what's fair to him. I care about Gus." Tears spilled down her cheeks. "If you love me at all, Charlotte, if I mean anything to you, promise me. Promise you won't tell him."

Charlotte clutched the medal in her fist. "I'll wait until Gus is at home. But that's all. That's all I can promise."

"You can't tell Dylan, either," Frances said, her mouth quivering. "Promise me."

"All right," Charlotte said, giving in to calm Frances down. "I promise I won't tell Dylan."

"What can't Charlotte tell me?" Dylan said, standing in the doorway.

CHAPTER TWENTY

THE THREE TURNED to stare at Dylan. Frances looked like she was going to cry.

"What is it?" he asked. "Is something else wrong with Gus? And why wouldn't you tell me?"

Frances shoved her fist in her mouth as she stared at him, tears streaming down her face. Kat moved closer to her mother and wrapped an arm around her shoulders. "Let's go, Mom. We need to get you home."

The two left without another word, although Kat turned and looked at him one more time. It felt as if she was studying him. Memorizing his face. He smiled cautiously. She looked stunned.

"What's going on?" he asked Charlotte.

She stood frozen in the middle of the room, her gaze locked on his, her expression devastated. Something small and silver dangled from a chain in her hand. He palmed the metal oval and brought it closer.

"This looks like my medal," he said. He touched his shirt, found the outline of it against his chest, then looked more closely at the one Charlotte held. "It's identical. Did you buy it after you saw mine?"

"No." She shook her head, her gaze never leaving his. "I've had this one for a long time."

Dylan frowned. "Where did you get it?"

She closed the chain and medal in her fist. Then, standing straighter, she hung it around her neck. "Gus gave it to me," she said. "The summer I became his first mate."

"Gus?"

She nodded, and suddenly he felt uneasy. "Where did Gus get it?"

"He ordered them from Scotland." She touched the medal around her neck. "St. Andrew the Apostle is the patron saint of fishermen."

Dylan felt the bottom drop out of his stomach as he stared at the medal on Charlotte's chest. "What did you promise Frances you wouldn't tell me, Charlotte? What was it you have to protect Gus from?"

"You know, Dylan. I can see it in your face."

"It's not possible," he said, dazed. "Gus can't be…he can't be my father."

"Why not?"

"Because he can't be." He would have known. Wouldn't he? Gus would have looked familiar. Dylan would have recognized him.

How could a man spend time with his father and not realize it?

"I think he is, Dylan. I think Gus is your father." She swallowed. "I thought you looked familiar the first time I saw you. You have Gus's eyes."

"I've been looking for my father for so long." He stared at Charlotte. "And you think it's Gus."

"Yes."

He stepped away from Charlotte. "You recognized the medal that night. The night we made love."

"Yes. I did." She faced him squarely.

"And you didn't tell me." His stomach twisted.

"I'm so sorry, Dylan. I didn't know what to do. I didn't know who to tell first."

"You should have told me."

"I couldn't! I'd promised Frances the reason you were here had nothing to do with Gus. I didn't know how she'd handle it. I had no idea if she even knew Gus had had an affair. And Gus had been so sick. He was doing better, but I was afraid of what the shock would do to him."

"Did you even think of me at all?"

"Of course I did. I've been thinking of nothing *but* you. Of how to tell you."

"Were you?" Her betrayal was a red-hot knife in his heart. "Is that why you promised Frances you wouldn't tell me?"

"That wasn't about you, Dylan. That was about Frances. About telling her what she needed to hear. Protecting her." She touched his arm, and he jerked away. "I had to promise her. I had to give her what she needed. I've loved her a lot longer than I've loved you."

"*Loved me?* What a joke. My God, Charlotte. How can you say you love me?" He swallowed around the huge lump in his throat. It was anger. That's all it was. "I trusted you with something I've never told anyone else. You betrayed my trust. And you have the nerve to say you love me?"

"I do love you."

The words twisted the knife, the pain so deep he wasn't sure he would survive it. "Don't say that." He turned away, unable to look at her. He stumbled over one of the plastic chairs lining the wall and kicked it out of his way. "Don't say you love me. You promised Frances, not me."

A nurse stepped into the waiting room, frowning. "Could you keep your voices down?" she said. "Our patients are very sick."

"Sorry," Charlotte murmured.

"Go to hell," Dylan snarled.

The nurse recoiled, then hurried away.

"Were you ever going to tell me, Charlotte? Or were you going to let me go back to Green Bay, thinking Stuart was my father?"

"Of course I was going to tell you." She looked shocked. "I wouldn't keep that from you."

"You already did. And now I might never get the chance to talk to my father." He paced the room, shoving the chair back into place. He picked up a magazine from the corner table and hurled it across the room. His hands itched for something else to do. Something besides touch Charlotte. "Gus might die before he knows he has a son and a granddaughter."

Tears poured down her face. "*No.* Gus is going to be fine. He *has* to be fine. The doctors said the surgery was a success. He'll wake up this evening."

"They don't know that for sure. It was brain

surgery. They won't know anything until he wakes up. *If* he does."

"I'm sorry, Dylan. So sorry. I made a mistake. I wish I could do it over again."

The afternoon sun focused a beam of light on her, turning her skin golden. God help him, he still wanted her. Blindly, he headed for the door.

"There aren't any do-overs."

"Please, Dylan, don't go."

She stood in front of the couch, holding out her hand to him. "Please. We can work through this. I love you."

"Love?" He shook his head. "You don't know the meaning of the word. If you loved me, you would have told me about Gus right away. You would have given me the chance to talk to him. It's too late to say you love me."

A security guard in a dark blue uniform appeared in front of him. "Is there a problem here, folks?"

"No problem, Rent-a-Cop." Dylan stormed past him and didn't look back. If he did, he might turn around. He might go back to Charlotte, gather her close and let her soothe his hurt.

And his fear.

He didn't need Charlotte. She'd betrayed him, then had the nerve to say she loved him. She'd found the thing that was dearest to him, his father, and withheld it from him. He didn't need that kind of love.

She'd made her choice. And it wasn't him.

And because of that choice, he hadn't gotten a chance to talk to Gus. His father, the man he'd searched for for so long, was lying unconscious in a hospital bed.

CHAPTER TWENTY-ONE

FIVE DAYS LATER, Charlotte sat on the swing in Frances's garden, hardly noticing the sunlight filtering through the leaves of the maple tree. As she rocked, trying to find the words she needed to say, the back door of the house slapped open.

"What are you doing hanging around here on a day like this?" Gus said as he walked slowly toward her. "There's nothing wrong with me. You shouldn't be taking time off. You're not going to make any money that way."

"Who said I was taking time off for you?" she said, standing and helping him into the swing. "I took a charter out first thing this morning, and I have another one scheduled for late this afternoon. So don't start thinking you're special or anything."

Gus smiled, but his face was still too pale. "You're all making me feel special," he said. "Even Smith. Did you see the article he wrote in the *Sturgeon Falls Herald?*"

"I haven't had a chance to look at the paper today," Charlotte said. "I was out early with the charter." She had glanced at the newspaper, but when she'd seen Dylan's name beneath the headline, she'd folded it over and set it aside. She'd read it when she was at home. Alone. Where no one would witness her tears.

"He did a damn fine job," Gus said. "The description he gave the sheriff was what caught the guy who clobbered me. And Smith nailed that developer. The guy who hit me has worked for the company for years." Gus snorted. "Damn coward. He had to sneak up behind me because he knew he couldn't beat me in a fair fight."

"Is that what Dylan said in the article?" Charlotte said, hiding a smile.

"Damn straight. He got it right."

"Of course he did. Dylan is a good reporter," Charlotte said. "He's passionate about what he does."

Gus arched an eyebrow. "That's not the only thing he's passionate about, is it?"

"Of course not. He's crazy about Hayley."

"I didn't mean Hayley, Charlotte."

"Then what did you mean? I don't know much about the rest of his life."

Gus scoffed. "Give it up, Charlotte. I saw the way he looked at you. And the way you looked back."

"That's over," she said, staring at Frances's flowers as the colors blurred together. "I should have listened to you. It never pays to date out-of-towners."

"He's from Green Bay, not the other side of the country. Smith isn't like that rat bastard Kyle Franklin. So why the hell is it over?"

Okay. This was the opening she needed. She rallied her courage and faced Gus.

"I made a mistake. A big one. That's why it's over."

"Over? That's stupid. Everyone makes mistakes."

"Not this big," Charlotte said, swallowing hard. "Dylan didn't tell you the reason he was here, looking into the Van Allen orchard."

"He said he was writing a story about it."

"No. That was never his reason for being here." She took a deep breath. "He was looking for his father. He thought it was Stuart Van Allen."

"That slick son of a bitch never could keep his pecker in his pants. So Van Allen got his mother pregnant?"

"That's the thing. It turns out Stuart isn't his father."

"Then who is?"

Charlotte licked her lips. "You, Gus. You're Dylan's father."

"What?" Gus frowned at her.

"You're Dylan's father," she repeated. "His mother worked at the orchard the summer you were there."

"Ruth Smith." His face became even more pale.

"Yes. Ruth was his mother."

"My God." His hand shook as he shoved it through his hair. "Ruthie had a baby?"

"Yes." She bit her lip to keep it from trembling. "She died before she could tell Dylan who you were. All he had was the St. Andrew the Apostle medal you'd given her, and an old label from a Van Allen orchard cherry crate."

"She kept the medal."

"She loved you very much," Charlotte said.

"Why didn't she tell me she was pregnant? Married or not, I would have done what was right. I would have supported her."

"I don't know," she said. "You'll have to ask Dylan."

"Dylan. My son," Gus said in wonder.

"Yes, Gus. Your son."

"And Hayley. I have a granddaughter." He smiled.

Charlotte's heart constricted. "She looks a little like Kat, doesn't she?"

He flopped against the seat and rubbed his hand over his eyes. "My God, Charlotte. What about Frances? I don't want to bring up that summer again. It took us too long to get over it."

"Frances already knows, Gus. She overheard me talking to you while you were in the hospital unconscious."

"And she hasn't said anything to me?"

"I made her promise not to. I'm the one who screwed up."

"How did you screw up?" Gus asked.

"I didn't tell you right away. And then Frances overheard me. Then Dylan overheard Frances." Her mouth quivered and she bit her lip. "I was trying to protect you and Frances, and instead I hurt everyone."

Gus's gaze narrowed. "How long have you known about this?"

She forced herself to look straight at Gus. "A few days before you were hurt."

"And you didn't say anything? To me or to Smith?"

"No. I told you it was a big mistake."

"Poor Charlotte," he said gently. "You were in an impossible position, weren't you?"

"Don't make excuses for me. Dylan said I betrayed him, and he's right. I knew how important this was to him."

He took her hand, and she clung to it. "Why didn't you come to me as soon as you knew?" he asked, without condemnation.

She looked away, ashamed of her motive, ashamed that fear had made her small and petty. She shrugged, searching for the right words.

"You were afraid, weren't you?"

She nodded, unable to speak.

"Afraid you'd lose me?"

Tears rolled down her face and she wiped them away impatiently. What was wrong with her? She'd cried more in the past week than she ever had. "Yes."

"That's just stupid," Gus said, shaking his head. "And you're not a stupid woman. You're the daughter of my heart, Charlotte. And you always will be. Did you think I was going to toss you aside because I found out I have another child? Don't be an ass."

"I know it's stupid," she said.

"Then knock it off. You hear me?" He cleared his throat. "Man in my condition doesn't need this kind of nonsense."

She hiccuped into a laugh. "What condition is that, Gus? I thought there was nothing wrong with you."

"That smart mouth of yours is going to get you into trouble one of these days," he growled.

Her smile disappeared. "It already has."

"If Smith is any kind of a man, he'll come around," Gus said. He suddenly looked old. "But first I have to make things right with Frances."

"She told me she already knew about the affair."

"I had to tell her. I loved her too much to keep that kind of secret from her." He rubbed a hand across his face. "But it was hard. We couldn't put it behind us until we had Kat. And Kat was a surprise. We didn't think we could have kids." He shook his head. "My poor Frances. It must have hurt her to find out I got another woman pregnant when we were struggling so much."

"She might surprise you," Charlotte said. "Frances loves you. And she's tougher than she looks."

"Yeah." Gus grimaced as he stood up. "Married to me, she had to be."

Charlotte watched Gus walk slowly toward the house. When he was inside, she let herself out of the yard, got in her truck and drove away.

CHARLOTTE WAS SITTING at her kitchen table, staring out the window, when a car pulled into her driveway. Dylan?

She hurried to the door, but it was Gus and Frances standing there.

Trying to smile, she ushered them inside. "Come in."

Frances enfolded Charlotte in her arms. "I'm

sorry. Sorry that you got caught in the middle of this. It was wrong of me to make you promise not to tell Gus or Dylan."

Charlotte allowed herself to relax into Frances, to soak up the love and acceptance. Then she eased away. "You're not angry?"

"Of course not," Frances said. "This whole mess was none of your doing."

"I promised you that Dylan had nothing to do with Gus."

Frances shook her head. "You didn't know that he did," she answered. "How could you?" She studied Charlotte, her expression tender. "Kat is my impulsive child. You were always the sensible one. So why are you blaming yourself for this?"

"I thought you'd be upset."

"And you didn't want to hurt me." She cupped Charlotte's face, and her hand felt cool. Healing. Like a mother's hand. "Charlotte. You're so dear to me. You're my daughter, you know, in every way that counts. How can you think I'd be upset with you for telling the truth? For doing the right thing?"

"I made a promise," she said. "And I broke it."

"A promise I had no business asking for. I knew I was being unreasonable. But I was beside myself." She linked her arm with Gus's. "I was so worried about him I couldn't think straight. I only wanted to protect him. And in the process, I hurt you."

"And you're not upset? That Dylan is Gus's son?"

"I forgave Gus for what happened that summer a long time ago. Knowing that the young woman had a child doesn't change that." She looked at her husband. "I'm just sad that he didn't get to see Dylan grow up." She smiled. "And I have a granddaughter. You and Kat are so darned independent, I'd almost given up on having grandchildren."

"Have you talked to Dylan?"

"After you left. He's coming over tonight," Gus answered. He hugged her, his embrace tight. "We wanted to talk to you first. To make sure you're okay."

She clung to Gus. "I'm going to be fine."

"You sure as hell don't look fine. When are you going to talk to Smith?"

She hadn't heard from Dylan since their confrontation at the hospital. "Don't worry about us," Charlotte said. She forced herself to smile. "And when are you going to stop calling him Smith and call him Dylan?"

"That was a silly name for a boy," Gus muttered. "What was Ruthie thinking?"

"You'd better not be saying that to Dylan tonight," Frances said, frowning. "Give him a few days to get to know you before you start snapping at him."

"Can't teach an old dog like me new tricks," he said. His face crinkled into a grin. "It wouldn't scare him off, anyway. He doesn't back down."

"Just like his father," Charlotte said, her heart aching.

"Is he stubborn like his father, too?" Frances asked. "Like you? I saw the way you and Dylan looked at each other. Don't substitute stubbornness for happiness. You belong together."

"Don't be ridiculous, Frances. I've only known Dylan for a couple of weeks. There's no such thing as love at first sight."

"Isn't there?" she said, looking at Gus and smiling. "You've never been a fool, Charlotte. Don't let your pride make a fool out of you now."

DYLAN ARRIVED AT the door of the Macauley home and paused, his hand on the doorbell. What should he say?

Hell, what should he do? Should he shake Gus's hand? Hug him? He had no idea. And what was he supposed to call him? Gus? Dad? His stomach tensed.

He didn't know how Gus felt about this. About finding out he had a son. Gus had called and said he'd talked to Charlotte. He'd asked Dylan to come over tonight. And that was it.

He should have asked Charlotte how Gus had taken the news. Asked her what to do.

No. He wasn't going to call Charlotte. The pain was a raw wound inside him, and talking to her would just make it bleed again.

Only an idiot would go back for more after he'd been betrayed once. He pressed the doorbell.

The door opened almost immediately. They'd probably seen his car and known he was standing on the porch like a total doofus. Plastering a smile on his face, he rubbed his suddenly sweating hands on his jeans. "Hi."

"Come in, Smith," Gus said.

Perversely, having Gus call him Smith made him relax. It was almost like nothing had changed.

But everything had.

As he stepped into the house, he looked around, curious. This is where his father lived. The man who had given him half his genes. Half of who he was.

The house was well-lived-in, with a pair of comfortable-looking plaid couches and a braided rug in the center of the floor. A recliner sat in one corner, facing the television. And there were pictures all over the walls. "These look like the pictures in Charlotte's house."

"They are," Gus said. "Frances painted them."

"They're beautiful, ma'am," he said. "All of them."

"Thank you, Dylan," Frances said. "And my name is Frances." She smiled. "Welcome."

"Thank you," he said, glancing at Gus. He'd imagined this scene so many times in the past. Meeting his father. Connecting with him in some mystical, woo-woo way. He'd never thought about what they'd say to each other.

"This is a hell of a development," Gus said, brushing his hand over his short, bristly hair. "Isn't it?"

"Yeah, I guess it is."

"A good one," Gus added. "Just strange as hell."

"Mr. Macauley, I didn't want to intrude on your life," Dylan said quickly. "I just needed to know where I came from. *Who* I came from."

Gus scowled. "What's this 'Mr. Macauley' crap? And who said you're intruding?"

"I know this isn't easy for you, or for your

family," Dylan said, wondering if he'd made a huge mistake by coming here tonight.

"Aw, hell." Gus took a step forward and engulfed Dylan in a bear hug. "You think I'm not thrilled to find out I have a son?" He pulled away and looked at Dylan. "Especially one who's as good a man as you? I am. Thrilled." He blinked fast. "I'm just not sure what to say."

"Me, either," Dylan admitted.

"Men," Frances muttered. "Neither of you has the sense God gave a goose." She pointed toward the recliner. "Sit," she told Gus. "And, Dylan, you sit on the couch there next to him. I'm going to go make some coffee. You two figure out if you've got a brain between you."

"Is she okay with this?" Dylan asked Gus when she'd gone. "It has to be kind of tough for her."

Gus looked down at his hands. "We had some problems after I told her about your mother that summer. But we worked it out. Now Frances is just as happy as I am. We feel as if we've won the lottery." Gus smiled. "And that daughter of yours is a bonus. We were beginning to think we'd never have a grandchild."

"Hayley is going to be so excited when I tell her. All I hear is 'Gus this' and 'Gus that.' To tell you the truth, I was beginning to feel like yesterday's news."

"You haven't told her yet?"

"I wanted to talk to you first. I didn't want to get her hopes up if you didn't want to be part of our lives."

"Damn right we do." He hesitated. "If that's what you want."

"Yes. I've been looking for you my whole life."

Gus studied Dylan's face. "You remind me of Ruthie," he said. "Your mouth, and the shape of your face."

"Charlotte said I have your eyes," Dylan said.

"Really?" Gus blinked hard.

Frances walked into the room carrying mugs of coffee. "Here you go. Hold on a minute."

She returned with a plate full of cookies. "You two have a lot to talk about. I'm going next door to talk to Dorothy. She wants me to come over and look at the pictures of her new grandson." She smiled. "It'll be a lot easier to take now, knowing that pretty soon I'll be able to show her pictures of our granddaughter."

Frances let herself out the front door and quiet descended on the house. Finally Gus said, "I loved your mother. Very much. It was wrong of me, but I loved her anyway. I wish she had told me she was pregnant."

"So do I, but we can't change the past."

"Nope, but you can tell me about it. I want to hear about you, and Ruthie, too." He pushed the coffee away and a little of it sloshed into the saucer. "What the hell was Frances thinking with the coffee and cookies? A man doesn't have cookies with his kid. You want a beer?"

"Yeah. A beer sounds good."

LATE THAT NIGHT, drinking his beer, Dylan asked, "How is Charlotte doing?"

"You haven't talked to her?" Gus raised an eyebrow and gave him a challenging look.

Dylan stared at his bottle. "I think you know I haven't."

"Then why are you asking?"

Dylan picked at the label. "I care about her."

Gus snorted. "The hell you do."

Dylan set the bottle down with a clink. "You may be my father, but that doesn't mean you can tell me how I feel."

"If you cared about Charlotte, you'd try to work things out. You'd talk to her." He sniffed. "You wouldn't sulk like a ten-year-old."

"I am not sulking."

"No?"

Dylan stretched his legs out, stared at his feet. "She's too important to me. I lo...I really care about her."

Gus sighed. "Hell, son, being in love is terrifying. Committing to a woman, trusting her with your life, that's pretty damn scary. Charlotte made a mistake. I'm sure you've made a few in your life. But the measure of a man is how he handles his mistakes. And how he forgives those of others."

"Yeah. I guess I have some thinking to do." Dylan eased off the couch. "And I've kept you up far too late. You need to get some rest."

"I've been doing nothing but resting since I got out of the hospital," Gus replied. "Talking to my son is more important." But his eyes were weary as he struggled to stand up.

"Yeah, but I've got a sister now," Dylan said, smiling. He helped Gus out of the chair. "I have it on good authority that she has a temper. She told me not to keep you up too late, and I don't want to cross her."

Gus walked him to the front door. "You coming back tomorrow?"

"You couldn't keep me away."

CHAPTER TWENTY-TWO

"HOW MANY ARE supposed to be on this charter?" Gus asked as he fiddled with the settings on her downriggers.

"Two couples, and I already set those," Charlotte answered, batting his hand away. "It'll be a nice, easy trip."

Gus scowled. "I'm damn sick of easy. I want to get back on my own boat. Run my own charters."

"And you can. As soon as Steve is back," she said easily. "I couldn't go out if you weren't helping me."

"He's not going to hurry back," Gus grumbled. "Not with you paying his salary while he's gone."

"Steve and his mom need the money," she said. "It's not easy to set up a new place."

"I'm proud of you, Charlotte," he said. "Kat told me what you said to Sheriff Godfrey. How you shamed him into arresting Lyle Jacobs."

She shrugged. "It was about time. And it made it easier for Helen to leave him. She's safe now, and that's what's important. And when Steve gets her settled, he'll be back working for me."

"Can't be soon enough for me," Gus answered.

"Yeah, I'm tough to work for," she said with a grin. "Everyone says so."

Gus snorted, but turned away to hide his own grin. He pulled out his box of lures and sat on the couch in the cabin to examine them. "Talk to Dylan lately?" he asked.

"Since you talk to him almost every day, you know I haven't."

"Call him, Charlotte."

"Did you tell him to call me?"

Silence.

"I already apologized," she said, slapping the cushion onto the cooler. "More than once. He made it abundantly clear he wasn't interested."

Gus dropped the lures. "That's the most bone-headed thing I've ever heard. Do you love him?"

"Yes," she said, staring out at the lake, pretending it was the reflected sunlight making her eyes water. "I do."

"Then what's wrong with you?" He shook his head. "I never thought you were a quitter, Charlotte."

The words stung. Just as he'd intended. "I'm not."

"Then tell him how you feel. Tell him until he believes you." Gus tugged at her hand, turning her to face him. "Life is too short," he said, his voice quiet. "Too short and too uncertain to throw away what you two have. And while you're at it, go visit your mother. It's not right that you two don't get along."

"You must have read my mind," she said. "I'm going to see her the day after tomorrow."

"Good. Finding Dylan has shown me how important family is. It's all that matters, and you can't take for granted they'll always be around. Because they won't."

"I know," she said. "I know."

TWO DAYS LATER she sat on the lumpy couch in her mother's run-down apartment in Green Bay. Everything was old and shabby, from the curtains to the frayed rug. But it was clean and neat. And there was no smell of stale cigarette smoke.

"It's not much," her mother said defensively. "But it's my own place. I can pay for it myself."

"It looks fine, Mom," Charlotte said. "Colorful." She smoothed her hand over the deep blue and yellow throw pillows.

Her mother lifted one shoulder. "I stopped smoking," she said. "And I haven't had a drink in six months and twenty-two days."

"You know exactly?"

"We keep track. It's part of the program."

"Congratulations. I'm really proud of you."

"Are you?" Her mother appeared wistful. "You never said that before, the other times I quit."

Her mother had never stayed sober for long. Maybe she'd needed more support, Charlotte thought with a pang of guilt. "I should have. I know how tough it is."

"It never goes away," her mom said. "The urge. I wake up in the middle of the night sometimes, wanting a drink. *Needing* a drink. Just one."

"What do you do when that happens?" Charlotte asked. She hesitated, then put her arm around her mother's shoulder.

"I call my sponsor in the group. I talk to her."

"You could call me. If you wanted to."

Her mother tilted her head. "I could," she said slowly. "I do believe you'd listen to me."

"I would, Mom. Call anytime."

Her mother eased away from Charlotte. "Tell me what you've been doing. Spending all your time fishing?"

The old resentment flared up, the anger that burned when her mother talked about the boat. But she didn't have to give in to the anger, she realized. And her mother wasn't attacking her. So she talked about the business, about the customers, about the fishing and the lake.

An hour later, her mother smiled when she finished another story. "You love that boat, don't you, honey?" she said.

"Yes, I do. I love what I do."

"It was wrong of me to be so against it. But it seemed like a hard job for a woman. I didn't want you to have such a hard life."

"I thought you wanted me to make more money," Charlotte said.

Her mother sighed. "That wouldn't have been a bad thing. But money doesn't buy happiness. Sometimes it just buys more misery. Look at my sister. She had all the money in the world, but her husband, Stuart, ran around on her."

Her mother glanced at her watch. "Oh, dear, look what time it is. I have to get ready for work. I'm sorry, honey. I don't want to push you out."

"It's okay, Mom. I understand."

She walked to the door and turned to find her mother right behind her. The older woman started to reach for her, then stopped. Charlotte stepped closer and hugged her.

"It was good to see you, Mom," she said. "I'll come back again soon."

"That would be nice." She smiled. "Thank you for coming, Charlotte."

Her mother shouldn't have to thank her for visiting, Charlotte thought regretfully. "I promise I'll be back, Mom. I'll see you soon."

In the narrow hall outside her mother's door, Charlotte took a deep breath. *I might be seeing you a lot sooner than you think, Mom.*

As she stepped into the sunlight and headed toward her truck, she pulled the directions to the Green Bay marina out of her pocket.

THE NEXT MORNING, she pulled into the Sturgeon Falls marina and looked around, drinking in the view. Dawn painted the water and the boats a pearly sheen of pink. The edge of the sun had just crept above the horizon, and the boats looked pale against the lightening sky. She was going to miss this place.

And thanks to Dylan's articles in the *Sturgeon Falls Herald,* the marina was going to be here for a while. The other charter captains had rallied around

Gus, and they'd told the development company they weren't interested in selling. Faced with the bad publicity from the attack on Gus, the company had quietly withdrawn its offer.

But Charlotte wasn't going to be here. She touched her purse, which held the paperwork for a lease at a marina in Green Bay. After Gus looked it over, she'd take it to an attorney before signing it. In October, at the end of the charter season, she'd move to Green Bay.

She wasn't going to let Dylan walk away from her without a fight.

She got out of her truck and stood looking around the marina that had been her second home since she was a child. As much as she'd miss it here, as much as she'd miss her friends and her family, she needed to be in Green Bay more. She needed to prove to Dylan she was serious, that she wanted a relationship with him.

That she was willing to do whatever it took.

As she walked down the pier toward the *Water Lily* in the weak light, she glanced at Gus's boat. It would be strange not to be able to stick her head in and ask him a question. Stranger still not to sit and talk to him like she usually did in the morning.

"Knock it off," she muttered. She wasn't moving to another planet. She'd only be an hour away.

"Still talking to yourself, Charlotte?"

Dylan was sitting on the dock against one of the posts, half-hidden in the shadows. The same place she'd seen him once before.

Her heart thumped against her ribs. "Dylan. What are you doing here?"

"Waiting for you," he said, standing up. "It took you long enough to get here."

"It's five a.m. My usual time."

"You weren't here yesterday at five a.m. Or anytime after that."

"You've been here since yesterday?"

"Yeah." He shoved his hands in his pockets. "Gus told me you were gone, but I figured you had to come home sometime."

Home. The word wrapped itself around her heart and squeezed. The marina wouldn't be home for much longer.

"Well, here I am," she said, suddenly self-conscious about her appearance. Instead of washing her hair this morning, she'd bundled it into a knot. Long strands had escaped and trailed down her neck. The jeans she'd grabbed were her oldest and rattiest pair, and the T-shirt was so worn it was verging on indecent.

"I need to talk to you," he said. "If that's okay."

"Why wouldn't I want to talk to you?"

"Maybe because I've been acting like an ass?"

The hard, tight ball that had lodged in her chest for the past two weeks began to loosen. "Let's move this to the boat," she said. Another vehicle had just pulled into the parking lot, and she knew the other captains would be arriving soon. "Where we can at least pretend there's some privacy."

She stepped into the cabin of the *Water Lily* and looked at Dylan. His eyes were tired and his clothes were wrinkled. His hair looked as if the wind had raked its fingers through it repeatedly. "You haven't been sitting on the pier all night, have you?" she asked, shocked.

"No. I slept for a few hours on Gus's boat."

She curled her hand into a fist to keep from touching him. "What's going on, Dylan?"

He moved a pen from one side of the sonar to the other and nudged a plastic chair back into place. He swallowed once, then squared around to face her. "I was a jerk at the hospital that day. A complete idiot. Gus said… Never mind what he said. Can you forgive me, Charlotte?"

Her heart plummeted. "What did Gus say?"

"It's not important. This isn't about Gus."

"It sounds like it *is* about Gus. I told him to keep his nose out of my business," she said, humiliated to think that Gus had browbeaten Dylan into apologizing. "Do you think an apology means anything when Gus told you to do it?"

"You think Gus is behind this? That I'm here because he told me to come see you?" He shook his head. "Believe me, he didn't have to tell me I'd been a jackass."

"Fine, you were a jackass and I was a liar. Okay?" She pushed past him, heading for the stairs. She didn't want to be standing in front of Dylan when she started to cry. She was so tired of crying. This was the last time.

Instead of the angry reply she expected, Dylan stepped in front of her. "Don't leave, Charlotte. I know you're still upset with me." He touched her face. "You have the right to be. But I won't let you push me away."

"What do you want, Dylan?"

"I want you, Charlotte. Just you. Remember what you said to me that day at the hospital? I want to hear you say it again."

"I don't know what you're talking about," she said. She knew exactly what he was talking about.

He took her hands and held them tightly. "When you told me you knew Gus was my father, that you'd known for a while, I was angry. He was in the hospital, hurt and unconscious, and I thought you'd cheated me out of a chance to know him."

She started to speak but he wasn't finished.

"More than angry, I was hurt that you chose Frances instead of me. That you promised her you wouldn't tell me. You shut me out, and the hurt was like nothing I've ever felt before—not when I got divorced, not when my stepfather was bullying me, not when my mother died. I was shocked by how much it felt like a betrayal. And that scared me to death."

"Why?" she asked.

"It made me realize how vulnerable I was. How much you could hurt me. How much power you had over me." He lifted his hand and brushed the hair away from her face. "I wanted to run, so I walked away. It was easier telling myself you'd betrayed me. And that's why I stayed away. I held on to my anger instead of facing my fear."

"And you're not afraid now?" She was almost afraid to hope.

"Sweetheart, I'm terrified. I'm afraid you'll tell me I've waited too long, that you're over me. That you didn't mean what you said that day."

"I meant it, Dylan."

"Thank God," he said. "I love you, Charlotte."

"I love you, too, Dylan."

He pulled her tight and she wrapped her arms around him. "I love you," she murmured, brushing her mouth over his.

He buried his face in her hair. "These past couple of weeks have been hell. I've been a miserable human being. Even Hayley told me to get a grip." He smiled at her. "She told me I was a stupid dork for dumping you."

"Wow," she said, swallowing around the lump in her throat. "That's a change."

"She told me you were cool. I told her she was a wise and observant child." He shifted his feet. "I think it helped that Annie stopped seeing the guy she'd dated a couple of times. Hayley felt more secure."

"I like Hayley. A lot."

"Even after she was so hostile to you?"

"She thought she was losing her father. I understood that. I was just as scared about losing Gus."

He kissed her and she melted into his arms. "I missed you so much," she whispered.

"I hate that I'm so far away from you," he said. "I'm going to…"

"Wait," she said, tearing herself away from him. She reached into her purse, pulled out the lease and handed it to him. "This is why I wasn't here yesterday."

He read the three pages, then looked up at her. "You signed a lease for a marina slip in Green Bay?"

"Not yet, but I'm going to. I wanted Gus and my attorney to look at it first. I'm going to do whatever it takes to convince you I love you. That I want to be part of your life. So I'm moving to Green Bay."

"You're leaving Sturgeon Falls?"

"You're more important than a town. My home is where you are."

He bent his head to kiss her, and she melted. She'd missed the taste of him, the strength of him beneath her hands. She'd missed the way he made her smile, and the way he'd made her feel.

"I can't let you move to Green Bay," he said, lifting his head. "I'll miss you too much."

"What do you mean?"

"I hope I can convince you to change your mind about that lease," he said. "Since I'm going to be living in Sturgeon Falls."

"What?"

He grinned, and her heart pounded. "I quit my job at the *Green Bay News-Gazette* and I'm going to work for Jimmy Lane at the *Sturgeon Falls Herald*. He wants to retire in a few years, so I'm going to buy him out."

"What have you done, Dylan?" She stared at him,

horrified. "You love your job. And you're good at it. I read some of your work." She'd read every one of his articles she could find on the Web.

"You did?" To her surprise, his cheeks reddened. "You read my stuff?"

"Of course I did." She draped her arms around his neck. "What do you think I did every night after my charters? I sat at home surfing the Web, looking for anything you'd written."

His mouth curved into a smile. "And here I was, picturing you out dancing every night."

"I hoped they'd help me figure out how to talk to you."

"I'm sorry, Charlotte." His smile faded. "I'm sorry I hurt you."

"I hurt you, too, Dylan." She ran her hands over his face. "But I'll never lie to you again. I promise."

"And I'll never walk away from you again. No matter how angry I am, no matter how upset, we'll work it out."

"Yes," she whispered, kissing him again.

As the kiss deepened, he moved his hands restlessly over her back, down to her hip. "I need you, Charlotte," he murmured, nipping at her ear. "I can't wait a moment longer. Please tell me you don't have a charter this morning."

"No charter." She eased away from him and pulled him toward the stairs. "Downstairs. Now."

A long time later, she raised herself on one elbow, looking down at Dylan lying in the bunk. Sunlight from the narrow window reflected off the water, slanted over him. "You don't have to move here, you know."

"And miss out on this?" He smiled lazily. "I'm counting on lots of mornings like this on your boat."

"They don't have to be in Sturgeon Falls, though."

"I *want* to be in Sturgeon Falls," he said. "I came here looking for my father and ended up finding my life. Finding you."

"I don't want you to uproot yourself for me."

"But it's okay for you to uproot yourself for me? Not going to happen." He kissed her nose. "Besides, you're not the only reason I want to be here. I want to spend time with my father. I want to get to know Frances and Kat. And I want Hayley to grow up with them."

"But Hayley lives in Green Bay."

"It's not that far. And I'm hoping I can convince Annie to move to Sturgeon Falls. She's not happy with her job in Green Bay, so maybe she'll look for one here."

"You have it all figured out."

"All except the most important part. When will you marry me?"

"As soon as possible."

"Thank God. I can't wait to begin our life together."

"It's not going to bother you to live so close to our family?"

"No. I want every single one of those messy family ties. Gus, Frances, Kat and I have a lot of years to make up." He nuzzled her neck, kissed her. "And I want a family with you."

"Don't let Gus or Frances hear you say that," she warned. "Grandchildren seems to be the magic word lately."

"At least Frances has a little subtlety. When I told Gus I was coming to talk to you, he told me he and Frances aren't getting younger and they want more grandchildren."

She groaned. "And you didn't tell him to mind his own business, did you? You probably laughed. In fact, you probably egged him on. You're going to be a very bad influence on him, Dylan."

"I'm planning on it. And I'm hoping he's a bad influence on me, too. I want to be just like Gus when I grow up." He tightened his arms around her.

"Cranky, stubborn and opinionated?"

He kissed her. "Comfortable with myself, proud of my kids and still madly in love with my wife."

"We'll make that happen." She touched the medal around his neck.

He closed his hand over hers, over the medal. "We can do anything, Charlotte, as long as we do it together."

Mediterranean Nights

Join the guests and crew of
Alexandra's Dream,
*the newest luxury ship to set sail
on the romantic Mediterranean, as they
experience the glamorous
world of cruising.*

*A new Harlequin continuity series
begins in June 2007 with*
FROM RUSSIA, WITH LOVE
by Ingrid Weaver.

*Marina Artamova books a cabin on the
luxurious cruise ship* **Alexandra's Dream**,
*when she finds out that her orphaned
nephew and his adoptive father are aboard.
She's determined to be reunited with the boy…
but the romantic ambience of the ship and
her undeniable attraction to a man
she considers her enemy
are about to interfere with her quest!*

Turn the page for a sneak preview!

Piraeus, Greece

"THERE SHE IS, Stefan. *Alexandra's Dream*." David Anderson squatted beside his new son and pointed at the dark blue hull that towered above the pier. The cruise ship was a majestic sight, twelve decks high and as long as a city block. A circle of silver and gold stars, the logo of the Liberty Cruise Line, gleamed from the swept-back smokestack. Like some legendary sea creature born for the water, the ship emanated power from every sleek curve—even at rest it held the promise of motion. "That's going to be our home for the next ten days."

The child beside him remained silent, his cheeks working in and out as he sucked furiously on his thumb. Hair so blond it appeared white ruffled against his forehead in the harbor breeze. The baby-sweet scent unique to the very young mingled with the tang of the sea.

"Ship," David said. "Uh, *parakhod.*"

From beneath his bangs, Stefan looked at the *Alexandra's Dream*. Although he didn't release his thumb, the corners of his mouth tightened with the beginning of a smile.

David grinned. That was Stefan's first smile this afternoon, one of only two since they had left the orphanage yesterday. It was probably because of the boat—according to the orphanage staff, the boy loved boats, which was the main reason David had decided to book this cruise. Then again, there was a strong possibility the smile could have been a reaction to David's attempt at pocket-dictionary Russian. Whatever the cause, it was a good start.

The liaison from the adoption agency had claimed that Stefan had been taught some English, but David had yet to see evidence of it. David continued to speak, positive his son would understand his tone even if he couldn't grasp the words. "This is her maiden voyage. Her first trip, just like this is our first trip, and that makes it special." He motioned toward the stage that had been set up on the pier beneath the ship's bow. "That's why everyone's celebrating."

The ship's official christening ceremony had been held the day before and had been a closed affair, with only the cruise-line executives and VIP guests invited, but the stage hadn't yet been disassembled. Banners bearing the blue and white of the Greek flag of the ship's owner, as well as the Liberty circle of stars logo, draped the edges of the platform. In the center, a group of musicians and a dance troupe dressed in traditional white folk costumes performed for the benefit of the *Alexandra's Dream*'s first passengers. Their audience was· in a festive mood, snapping their fingers in time to the music while the dancers twirled and wove through their steps.

David bobbed his head to the rhythm of the mandolins. They were playing a folk tune that seemed vaguely familiar, possibly from a movie he'd seen. He hummed a few notes. "Catchy melody, isn't it?"

Stefan turned his gaze on David. His eyes were a striking shade of blue, as cool and pale as a winter horizon and far too solemn for a child not yet five. Still, the smile that hovered at the corners of his mouth persisted. He moved his head with the music, mirroring David's motion.

David gave a silent cheer at the interaction. Hopefully, this cruise would provide countless opportunities for more. "Hey, good for you," he said. "Do you like the music?"

The child's eyes sparked. He withdrew his thumb with a pop. *"Moozika!"*

"Music. Right!" David held out his hand. "Come on, let's go closer so we can watch the dancers."

Stefan grasped David's hand quickly, as if he feared it would be withdrawn. In an instant his budding smile was replaced by a look close to panic.

Did he remember the car accident that had killed his parents? It would be a mercy if he didn't. As far as David knew, Stefan had never spoken of it to anyone. Whatever he had seen had made him run so far from the crash that the police hadn't found him until the next day. The event had traumatized him to the extent that he hadn't uttered a word until his fifth week at the orphanage. Even now he seldom talked.

David sat back on his heels and brushed the hair from Stefan's forehead. That solemn, too-old gaze locked with his, and for an instant, David felt as if he looked back in time at an image of himself thirty years ago.

He didn't need to speak the same language to understand exactly how this boy felt. He knew what it meant to be alone and powerless among strangers, trying to be brave and tough but wishing with every fiber of his being for a place to belong, to be safe, and most of all for someone to love him....

He knew in his heart he would be a good parent to Stefan. It was why he had never considered halting the adoption process after Ellie had left him. He hadn't balked when he'd learned of the recent claim by Stefan's spinster aunt, either; the absentee relative had shown up too late for her case to be considered. The adoption was meant to be. He and this child already shared a bond that went deeper than paperwork or legalities.

A seagull screeched overhead, making Stefan start and press closer to David.

"That's my boy," David murmured. He swallowed hard, struck by the simple truth of what he had just said.

That's my *boy*.

"I CAN'T BE PATIENT, RUDOLPH. I'm not going to stand by and watch my nephew get ripped from his country and his roots to live on the other side of the world."

Rudolph hissed out a slow breath. "Marina, I don't like the sound of that. What are you planning?"

"I'm going to talk some sense into this American kidnapper."

"No. Absolutely not. No offence, but diplomacy is not your strong suit."

"Diplomacy be damned. Their ship's due to sail at five o'clock."

"Then you wouldn't have an opportunity to speak with him even if his lawyer agreed to a meeting."

"I'll have ten days of opportunities, Rudolph, since I plan to be on board that ship."

* * * * *

*Follow Marina and David as they
join forces to uncover the reason behind
little Stefan's unusual silence, and the
secret behind the death of his parents....*

Look for
From Russia, With Love
by Ingrid Weaver
in stores June 2007.

Silhouette®
Romantic
SUSPENSE

**Sparked by Danger,
Fueled by Passion.**

*This month and every month look for
four new heart-racing romances
set against a backdrop of suspense!*

Available in June 2007

Shelter from the Storm
by **RaeAnne Thayne**

A Little Bit Guilty
(Midnight Secrets miniseries)
by **Jenna Mills**

Mob Mistress
by **Sheri WhiteFeather**

A Serial Affair
by **Natalie Dunbar**

Available wherever you buy books!

REQUEST YOUR FREE BOOKS!
2 FREE NOVELS PLUS 2 FREE GIFTS!

HARLEQUIN®

Super Romance®

Exciting, emotional, unexpected!

YES! Please send me 2 FREE Harlequin Superromance® novels and my 2 FREE gifts. After receiving them, if I don't wish to receive any more books, I can return the shipping statement marked "cancel." If I don't cancel, I will receive 6 brand-new novels every month and be billed just $4.69 per book in the U.S., or $5.24 per book in Canada, plus 25¢ shipping and handling per book and applicable taxes, if any*. That's a savings of close to 15% off the cover price! I understand that accepting the 2 free books and gifts places me under no obligation to buy anything. I can always return a shipment and cancel at any time. Even if I never buy another book from Harlequin, the two free books and gifts are mine to keep forever.   135 HDN EEX7   336 HDN EEYK

Name _____ (PLEASE PRINT) _____

Address _____ Apt. _____

City _____ State/Prov. _____ Zip/Postal Code _____

Signature (if under 18, a parent or guardian must sign) _____

Mail to the **Harlequin Reader Service®:**
IN U.S.A.: P.O. Box 1867, Buffalo, NY 14240-1867
IN CANADA: P.O. Box 609, Fort Erie, Ontario L2A 5X3

Not valid to current Harlequin Superromance subscribers.

Want to try two free books from another line?
Call 1-800-873-8635 or visit www.morefreebooks.com.

* Terms and prices subject to change without notice. NY residents add applicable sales tax. Canadian residents will be charged applicable provincial taxes and GST. This offer is limited to one order per household. All orders subject to approval. Credit or debit balances in a customer's account(s) may be offset by any other outstanding balance owed by or to the customer. Please allow 4 to 6 weeks for delivery.

Your Privacy: Harlequin is committed to protecting your privacy. Our Privacy Policy is available online at www.eHarlequin.com or upon request from the Reader Service. From time to time we make our lists of customers available to reputable firms who may have a product or service of interest to you. If you would prefer. we not share your name and address, please check here. ☐

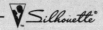

SPECIAL EDITION™

COMING IN JUNE

HER LAST
FIRST DATE

by *USA TODAY* bestsellling author
SUSAN MALLERY

After one too many bad dates, Crissy Phillips
finally swore off men. Recently widowed,
pediatrician Josh Daniels can't risk losing his
heart. With an intense attraction pulling them
together, will their fear keep them apart?
Or will one wild night change everything...?

Sometimes the unexpected
is the best news of all....

COMING NEXT MONTH

#1422 COULDA BEEN A COWBOY • Brenda Novak
A Dundee, Idaho story

Tyson Garnier is a stranger to Dundee—and to his own infant son. The baby was neglected by his mother, so Tyson paid her off to get full custody. Now he needs a temporary nanny, and Dakota Brown is perfect. She's completely unlike the kind of women Tyson usually attracts. She's poor, a little plain, a hard worker. Who would've guessed he'd find himself falling for someone like *that?*

#1423 BLAME IT ON THE DOG • Amy Frazier
Singles…with Kids

An out-of-control mutt. A preteen son. Dog trainer Jack Quinn. These are the males in Selena Milano's life. The first two she loves. The third? Who knows? But he sure does make things interesting.

#1424 HIS PERFECT WOMAN • Kay Stockham

Dr. Bryan Booker is the perfect man. Ask almost every woman in town—including some of the married ones. Even Melissa York is hard-pressed to deny Bryan's charms. Not that she can afford to be interested…since he's already said the only way she can work for him is if they keep everything professional. But is he going to remember that?

#1425 DAD FOR LIFE • Helen Brenna
A Little Secret

Lucas Rydall is looking for redemption. His search leads him to his ex-wife, Sydney Mitchell—and the son he didn't know he had. But his discovery puts them all in danger. To save his family, Lucas must put aside his fears and become the man his family needs.

#1426 MR. IRRESISTIBLE • Karina Bliss

Entrepreneur Jordan King is handsome and charismatic, and he's used to getting any woman he wants. Until journalist Kate Brogan catches his eye—and refuses to give in to her obvious feelings for him. Because the way she sees it, he's just like her father: a no-good philanderer at the mercy of his passions. So all Jordan has to do is convince her he's utterly irresistible.

#1427 WANTED MAN • Ellen K. Hartman

Nathan has a secret. One he has to hide—which means leaving his old life behind and not telling a soul who he really is. But how can a man with any honor even think about getting involved with a woman as wonderful as Rhian MacGregor?